created by John Layman & Rob Guillory

written & lettered by
John Layman
drawn & colored by
Rob Guillory

Color Assists by Taylor Wells

CHEW, VOL. 5: MAJOR LEAGUE CHEW. First printing. April 2011. Published by Image Comics, Inc. Office of publication: 2134 Allston Way, 2nd Floor, Berkeley, CA 94704. Printed in the U.S.A. For information regarding the CPSIA on this printed material call: 203-595-3636 and provide reference # RICH – 432241

International Rights Representative: Christine Meyer (christine@gfloystudio.com ISBN: 978-1-60706-523-4

Dedications:

JOHN: To Tom Peyer, because he likes baseball. And balls.

ROB: To Jim Mahfood, for letting a young (and annoying) Rob send him mini-comics in 2002. Thanks for being a cool dude.

Thanks:

Taylor Wells, *for the coloring assists.*
Tom B. Long, *for the logo.*
Comicbookfonts.com, **for the fonts.**

And More Thanks:

Paul Benjamin, Lance Curran, Aris Ilipoulous, Robert Kirkman and Christine Meyer, as well as Indispensible Image-ites Drew, Tyler, Branwyn, eric, Todd, Sarah, Jonathan and Emily. Also: Kim Peterson and April Hanks. Also: Patrick Swayze.

Olive Chu's wardrobe provided by Threadless.com
Designs by **Glenn Jones** *and* **Jason LaRose**

Chapter 1

MONDAY.
HOOKY'S
BER
SHOP
HOOKY.
SUN
SCIENTISTS TEST PROVE:
BEST DAY EVAR!!
A BEAUTIFUL DAY.

A BEAUTIFUL, *BEAUTIFUL* DAY.
A BEAUTIFUL, BEAUTIFUL, BEAUTIFUL, *BEAUTIFUL* DAY.
EGG
A GREAT BIG BEAUTIFUL, WONDERFUL, STUPENDOUS, ABSOLUTELY *FANTABULOUS* DAY.
CHU FIRED!! PARTY @ APPLEBEE'S
MISSING
FDA
YOU'RE *FIRED*.

LET'S BACK UP A BIT.
FDA OFFICES
APPLEBEE 5-C
LEUNG 4-B
HOLLOWAY 14-J
THRACE --
PAIK 13-G
FOX 23-E
VALENZANO 5-B
ROSLIN PH
LINUS 3-A
COLBY 5-A
ADAMA 7-C
BISHOP B
LOCKE 15-D
BELL --
CHU - HELL.
ER... EXCUSE ME.
YOU'RE SITTING AT MY DESK.
munch munch
TPS REPORT
BRING YOUR OWN STAPLES! BUDGET CUTS!! -A
TOILET PAPER FOR OFFICE USE ONLY!
CHEEZ.
RANCH BITS.
CRAKLIN
PHAT-O
VOORHEES
SOYBEAN OIL, GLYCEROL, WHEAT PROTEIN ISOLATE, SODIUM PYROPHOSATE...
SHRUG
LISTEN:
YOU'RE SITTING AT MY DESK.
NO, OFFICER CHU.
SPECIAL AGENT VORHEES IS SITTING AT HIS DESK.
OUR NEW RECRUIT. OUR BEST AND BRIGHTEST.
WHILE YOU... OFFICER CHU...
YOU...
HERE COMES THE "FIRED" PART.

WHAT DO YOU MEAN "FIRED"?
WELL, TRANSFERRED, IF YOU WANT TO GET TECHNICAL.
BUT YOU'RE OUT OF MY OFFICE, OUT OF MY HAIR, OUT OF MY LIFE.
AND AS FAR AS I'M CONCERNED --AND THE FDA-- THAT MEANS JUST ONE THING.
YOU'RE FIRED.
YOU'LL BE REPORTING TO THE MUNICIPAL TRAFFIC DIVISION IN THE MORNING.
TRAFFIC?!?!
MMM-HMM. AND NOW SECURITY WILL ESCORT YOU FROM THE PREMISES.
IDEA: JUMP TO CONCLUSIONS MAT. -A.
FDA
SO LONG!
SAYONARA!
AU REVOIR!
AUF WIEDERSEHEN!

YOU TOO, FUCKO.
YOU'RE OUTTA HERE.
HEY, HOLD ON NOW. MAYBE WE SHOULD SLOW DOWN, THINK THINGS THROUGH.
FDA
YOU AND ME, WE HAD SOMETHING GOOD FOR A WHILE THERE, RIGHT?
MAYBE WE CAN TALK THIS OVER?
MAYBE OVER DINNER?
YOUR TRANSFER PAPERS.
GET OUT.
FUMP
WAITA-MINUTE.
YOU'RE TRANSFERRING ME WHERE?!?!

TUESDAY.
...
THIS UNIFORM MAKES ME LOOK LIKE A JACKASS.
NON-SENSE.
YOU LOOK VERY...
VERY...
UM...
WELL, TRY TO HAVE A GOOD DAY *ANYWAY*.

HERE'S TONY CHU.
IT'S TONY CHU'S FIRST DAY AS AN ENFORCEMENT OFFICER IN THE MUNICIPAL TRAFFIC DIVISION OF THE CITY POLICE, ONE OF THE LEAST POWERFUL LAW ENFORCEMENT AGENCIES IN THE WORLD.
HERE'S WHY HE WAS REASSIGNED:

TONY CHU IS *CIBOPATHIC*.
THAT MEANS HE CAN TAKE A BITE OF A TOMATO, AND GET A FEELING IN HIS HEAD ABOUT WHAT VINE IT GREW ON, WHAT PESTICIDES WERE USED ON THE CROP, AND WHEN IT WAS HARVESTED.
OR HE CAN EAT A BITE OF VEAL, AND FLASH ONTO SOMETHING *ELSE* ENTIRELY.
HIS *PREVIOUS* BOSS, MIKE APPLEBEE, HAD AN IMMEDIATE AND INTENSE HATRED FOR TONY--
AGENT CHU!
--AND WORKED *NONSTOP* TO GET HIM REMOVED AS A SPECIAL AGENT FOR THE *FDA*.
THIS IS LT. MARSHALL MELLO.
TONY'S *NEW* BOSS.
WELCOME!!!
AND HE HAS A CONSIDERABLY *DIFFERENT* OPINION OF TONY.

I'M LIEUTENANT MELLO. SUCH A PLEASURE TO MEET YOU!
PARK LIKE YOU MEAN IT!
WE ARE SO, SO, SO VERY HONORED TO HAVE YOU HERE, SPECIAL AGENT CHU.
IT'S JUST OFFICER CHU NOW, I SUPPOSE.
P'SHAW! ONCE A SPECIAL AGENT, ALWAYS A SPECIAL AGENT.
WELCOME TO THE TEAM, ANTHONY!!
EVERY-BODY, YOUR ATTENTION, PLEASE!
THIS IS HIM. ER, HE. THE GUY I WAS TELLING YOU ABOUT.
ANTHONY CHU.
ER, JUST "TONY" IS FINE.
WET!
I ♡ my PRIUS!
NEEDS MORE COW-BELL!
Buy CAT FOOD
PARKING.
HE'S WORKED FOR THE FDA. HE'S WORKED ALONGSIDE THE USDA. WITH NASA.
A REAL HERO, THROUGH AND THROUGH.
HE EVEN DID A STINT BEFORE THAT ON THE POLICE VICE SQUAD.
NOW HE'S WITH US.
AND I, FOR ONE, COULD NOT BE HAPPIER.

ON THE JOB.
LIFE IS HELL
SAD GOTH 4 LIFE!
TICKET
CITY
CREMINI.
NO PARKING
WTF ?
EGGS
THEY LIE

YOU KNOW YOU'RE NOT SUPPOSED TO PARK IN FRONT OF A FIRE HYDRANT, RIGHT?
AW, MAN.
CLUCK YOU
LOOK, I'LL LET YOU OFF WITH A WARNING--
--BUT I'M PRETTY SURE YOU'RE NOT OLD ENOUGH FOR THAT BEER, SO I'M GONNA HAVE TO CONFISCAT--
HEY, I RECOGNIZE YOU--
--AREN'T YOU THAT FDA GUY?
LAYMAN BOOZE
LAYMAN LIQUOR
LAYMAN HOOCH
WHAT HAPPENED, YOU GET BUSTED DOWN TO METER MAID OR SOME-THING?
HAW! NICE KILT!
ANYBODY EVER TELL YOU THAT UNIFORM MAKES YOU LOOK LIKE A JACKASS?
HAW HAW HAW!
EGG
THAT IS, I WAS GOING TO LET YOU OFF WITH A WARNING.
DWEET DWEET DWEET
HOLD ON A SECOND... I NEED TO TAKE THIS.
SUN
CLUCK YOU.
LAYMAN HOOCH
100% PROOF

IT'S ROSEMARY, TONY.
OLIVE'S *MISSING*.
I WASN'T GOING TO CALL YOU, BECAUSE I *KNOW* SHE'S NOT WITH YOU.
BUT SHE HASN'T BEEN HOME SINCE THURSDAY, AND I'M STARTING TO GET *REALLY* WORRIED.
SHE HASN'T BEEN TO SCHOOL AND NONE OF HER FRIENDS HAVE SEEN HER.
OLIVE'S DONE THIS *BEFORE*, ROSEMARY-- *REPEATEDLY*.
WASH ME...
DAMN DA MAN!
COEXIST
I'VE CALLED AROUND. ALL OF HER FRIENDS. ALL OF THEIR FAMILIES.
NOBODY'S *SEEN* HER. NOBODY KNOWS WHERE SHE *IS*.
YOU'VE GOT ALL THAT *FDA POWER*. YOU NEED TO *USE* IT AND *FIND* HER, TONY.
ER... ABOUT MY *FDA* JOB.
THERE'S BEEN A COUPLE OF *CHANGES*.
I DON'T *NEED* THIS SORT OF STRESS IN MY LIFE, LITTLE BROTHER.
THIS IS *YOUR* DAUGHTER WE'RE TALKING ABOUT.
YOUR RESPONSIBILITY.
LOOK, ROSE, I'LL POKE AROUND AND SEE WHAT I CAN COME UP WITH--
--BUT I'M SURE YOU'VE GOT *NOTHING* TO WORRY--
CLICK
TONY?
WHAT THE FUCK ?!?!
VROOOOOM

@#&%
FRRR
FRRROOOOMMMM
THIRD NATIONAL BANK
WHAT THE HELL HAPPENED HERE?
AAA
DO N

NOT REAL SURE.
GOD-DAMN UGLY IS WHAT IT WAS.
BUT WE DIDN'T GET ANY UNIFORMS ON THE SCENE 'TIL AFTER IT WAS OVER.
NEVER MIND...
WHAT ARE YOU--
...I THINK I GOT A HANDLE ON THIS.

AND THIS IS WHERE THE GETAWAY CAR PULLED OUT?
THINK SO. LONG GONE BEFORE WE GOT HERE.
IS HE LICKING MOTOR OIL?
MAN, THOSE TRAFFIC DIVISION DUDES TAKE THEIR SHIT SERIOUSLY.
DALTONS GARAGE
BANK PLANS
YEAH, I GOT THIS ONE.

SOON, IN A WAREHOUSE HIDEOUT ACROSS TOWN.
HOW MUCH?
I'M NO MATHEMATICIAN, BUT I'D SAY THIS QUALIFIES AS A METRIC SHIT-TON.
KNOCK KNOCK KNOCK
WHAT THE--
WHO IS IT?
DONT FORGET TO FLUSH BEFORE LEAVING!
MAY 93
MUNICIPAL TRAFFIC OFFICER CHU, SIR.
THERE'S A MOTORCYCLE OUT HERE ILLEGALLY PARKED. IS IT YOURS?

JUST SOME NOSY TRAFFIC COP.
HE DOESN'T *KNOW* ANYTHING.
KEEP COOL. FEED 'IM SOME STORY.
HUMOR HIM... THEN GET *RID* OF HIM.
SORRY, OFFICER, I DON'T KNOW ANYTHING ABOUT AN ILLEGALLY PARKED MOTORCYCLE.
EXIT
YEAH, ME *NEITHER*.
CLOSED. OUT OF BIZ-NESS. (MAYBE FOREVER.)
KZZZZZAPPPPP
DROP YOUR WEAPONS...

SKRASHHH
BRAKRAM!
SWAT
BUST
UZI
CHOPPER
...YOU'RE *BUSTED*.

END OF SHIFT.
MUNICIPAL TRAFFIC HQ
"PLEASE DON'T HATE US... IT'S THE LAW."
WE DIDN'T MAKE THE LAW. SORRY!
SERIOUSLY C'MON...
AGENT CHU!
CHU, T.
THERE HE IS--OUR CONQUERING *HERO!*
I JUST *KNEW* YOU WERE GONNA BE GREAT HERE, SPECIAL AGENT CHU.
I JUST KNEW IT!
THREE CHEERS FOR OUR OWN SPECIAL AGENT --OUR OWN *SUPER* SPECIAL AGENT-- ANTHONY CHU!
HIP HIP HOORAY!
HIP HIP HOORAY!

EVENING.
TakaTakaTak TakaTaka
MORE BEETS
SO.
HOW WAS YOUR DAY?
FOODIE!
BE HAPPY TONY!
IT...
...WASN'T BAD...
IT WAS ACTUALLY... GOOD?
I CAN'T BELIEVE IT...
...BUT I THINK MAYBE I MIGHT ACTUALLY LIKE THIS JOB.

WEDNESDAY.
KaWHAMM
SKPOW
TICKET:
FINE:
ADD $5 TO FINE OUT OF SPITE!
RECEIPT
WHAM
FWAM
CRACK
END MAJOR LEAGUE CHEW: CHAPTER I

Chapter 2

THE BALL THAT SHOOK THE WORLD.
BIG GAME SHUT OUT!!
HERO!
FOUND DEAD! MYSTERY
TOOLS
ROB!

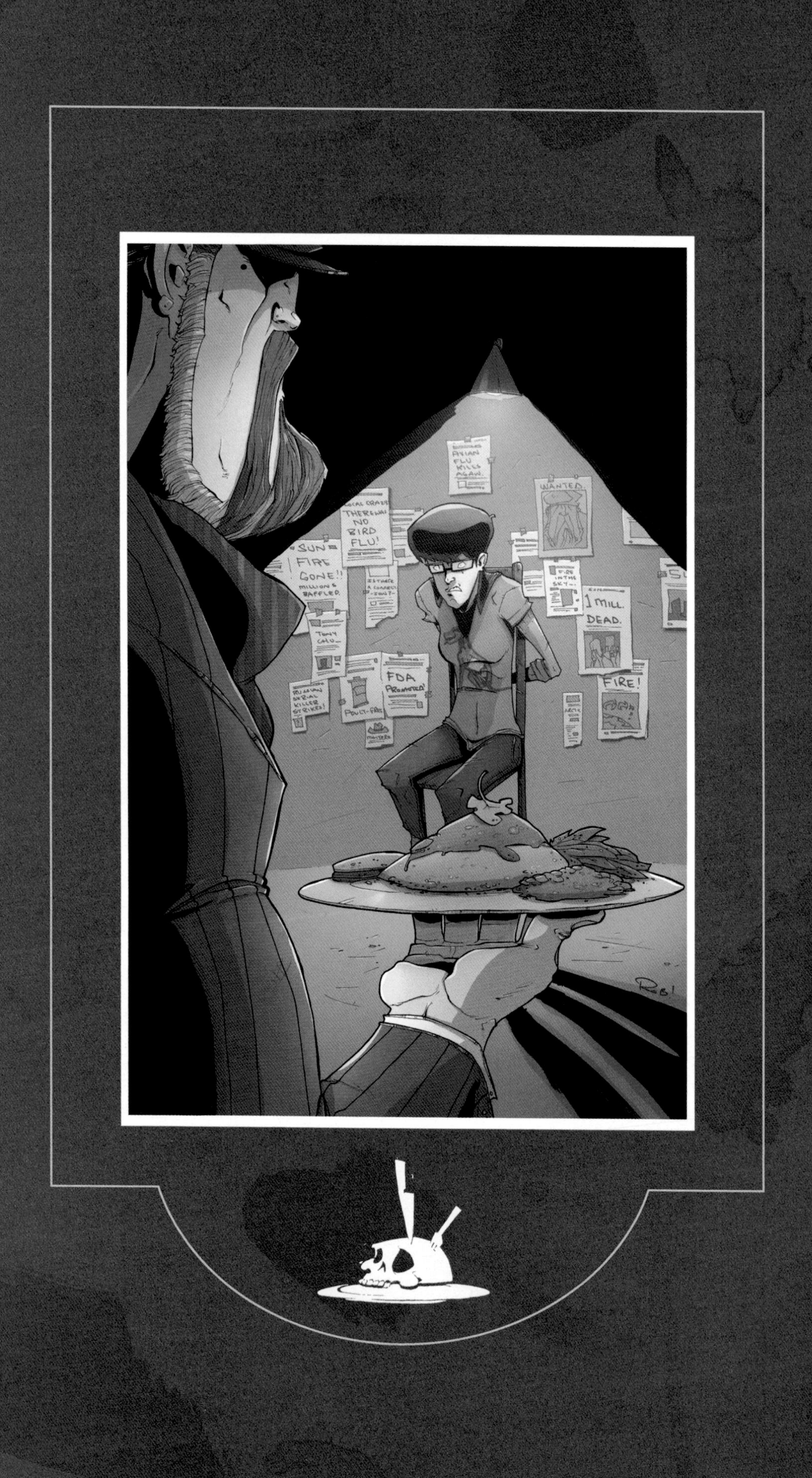
AVIAN FLU KILLS AGAIN.
WANTED.
LOCAL CRAZY: THERE WAS NO BIRD FLU!
SUN FIRE GONE!! MILLIONS BAFFLED.
IS THERE A CONNECTION?
FIRE IN THE SKY...
1 MILL. DEAD.
TONY CHU...
FDA PROMOTED!
RUSSIAN SERIAL KILLER STRIKES!
POULT-FREE
FIRE!
ROB!

PROLOGUE.
LATER THAT SAME DAY.
LEMME GUESS:
THE LIL' CHU GAL AIN'T *COOPERATING* SO WELL, IS SHE?

YOUR ASSESSMENT IS NOT ENTIRELY INCORRECT, CAESAR.
OUR YOUNG MISS CHU IS A VERY WILLFUL CHILD.
A VERY STUBBORN CHILD.
BUT ONE TO WHOM I HOPE I AM FINALLY GETTING THROUGH TO.
AGAIN, MISS CHU, I APOLOGIZE FOR THE... UNCONVENTIONAL AND NO DOUBT UNPLEASANT MEANS OF INTRODUCTION.
BUT WE BOTH KNOW YOU WOULD NOT HAVE ACCOMPANIED ME WILLINGLY.
AND I ASSURE YOU, DESPITE APPEARANCES TO THE CONTRARY, ULTIMATELY, THIS IS FOR YOUR OWN GOOD.
AND TO YOUR GREAT BENEFIT.
I KNOW YOU TO BE EXTRAORDINARY, MY DEAR--
--AND I CAN HELP YOU TO ACHIEVE ALL YOU HAVE THE POTENTIAL TO--
--BUT YOU HAVE TO ALLOW ME TO.
ASSENT TO MY OFFER OF TUTELAGE--
--AND I WILL ENDEAVOR TO BESTOW FULLY UPON YOU THE ACCUMULATION OF MY MANY YEARS OF EXPERIENCE, KNOWLEDGE AND WISDOM.
BUT TO DO THIS I MUST FIRST ASCERTAIN EXACTLY WHAT YOU ARE CAPABLE OF--
--AND THE BOUNDARIES OF YOUR TALENT.
IT IS A SIMPLE BARGAIN.
YOU EAT.
YOU SEE.
YOU SHARE.
AND I TEACH.

OLIVE CHU HAS BEEN KIDNAPPED.

SHE WAS AMBUSHED, KNOCKED OUT, BROUGHT TO A REMOTE LOCATION, AND BOUND SECURELY.

HER CAPTOR INTENDS TO *FEED* HER FROM A MENU OF *HIS* CHOOSING, TO FIND OUT WHAT OLIVE CAN SEE, IN ORDER TO *LEARN* FROM HER.

NOT COOPERATING AT ALL, CAESAR.
LOOKS LIKE YOU COULD USE A BREAK, MASON.
HERE. BROUGHT YOU A CUP O' COFFEE.
THANK YOU, CAESAR, BUT NO. IT'S A LITTLE LATE IN THE DAY--
LET ME REPHRASE.
YOU NEED TO BE TRYIN' THIS COFFEE.
EH? WHAT IS THIS?
HOPIN' YOU COULD TELL ME, BIG MAN.
SSSSIP
HMMM.
COFFEE IS AWESUM!
JUMPING BEAN CAFE!
BEANS PICKED IN ORSOSI, COSTA RICA, ROASTED LOCALLY...
...JUMPING BEAN CAFE, CORNER OF OAK AND 34TH ST.
HINT OF ECUADORIAN DARK CHOCOLATE.
DUSTING OF INDONESIAN CINNAMON.
DASH OF CATALONIAN CHICORY.
AND... AND...
MALEVOLENCE!!
YOU LIKE SLEEP?? US EITHER. THAT'S WHY WE PUT CRACK
END PROLOGUE.

EARLIER THAT SAME DAY.
THE CASE OF THE CIRCUS CLOWN CHICKEN SMUGGLERS.
AGENT VALENZANO, IT'S AGENT CHU. ER...*OFFICER* CHU, I MEAN.
COULD YOU CALL ME BACK, PLEASE?
THE MYSTERY OF THE MURDERED MASCOT.
CHARLESTON CHICKENS
HOME
AWAY
CHICKENS GET CHOKED!! XXX
FLUFFY
CAESAR. IT'S TONY. TONY CHU.
GIMME A CALL, WOULD YOU?

AMISH ICE CREAM ENTOMBMENT.
I NEED A FAVOR, CAESAR.
MY DAUGHTER, OLIVE... SHE'S GONE MISS-ING.
FAT CAMP COUP D'ÉTAT.
Richard Simmons was RIGHT.
SORRY TO BOTHER YOU AGAIN, CAESAR.
I NEED YOU TO PULL A FEW STRINGS FOR ME, USE YOUR FDA CONNEC-TIONS.
CALL ME!!

--PROBABLY JUST MY SISTER PANICKING OVER NOTHING.
--BUT I KNOW THE FDA MISSING PERSONS DATABASE IS MORE COMPREHENSIVE THAN WHAT I HAVE ACCESS TO IN TRAFFIC DIVISION.
THANKS A BUNCH, CAESAR. PLEASE CALL ME BACK WHEN YOU GET THE CHANCE.
<SIGH.>
AGENT VALENZANO!
YOU'RE NOT USING AN FDA PHONE FOR PERSONAL CALLS, ARE YOU?
ER, SORRY, DIRECTOR APPLEBEE.
I WAS, UH, JUST CHECKING MY MESSAGES.
NOT TO WORRY. IT'S A NEW DAY HERE AT THE FDA.
A GREAT BIG BEAUTIFUL, WONDERFUL DAY.
IT'S THAT DAMN CHU.
KEEPS CALLIN' 'CAUSE HE THINKS HIS DAUG--
TONY CHU?!?
NO MORE PERSONAL CALLS.
STOMP
STOMP
STOMP

STOMP
STOMP
STOMP
THE SHIT STACK...
FUMP
GET TO WORK.
WORK:
CALF-KILLER 3000. OUR SHOES WILL DESTROY YOUR CALVES.
JUMPING BEAN CAFE!
CAFFEINE WILL MAKE YOU JUMP, JUMP!!!
THE MERCURY SUN

GOTTA APOLOGIZE TO YOU 'BOUT THE LAST COUPLE DAYS.
JOB USED TO BE A LOT MORE CHILL. FOR ME, ANYWAY, 'CAUSE APPLEBEE ALWAYS SENT CHU AND COLBY ON THE SHIT ASSIGN-MENTS.
AND NOW THEY GONE AND WE GOTTA PICK UP TH' SLACK.
CAFFEINE WILL KILL YA!!
YOU AIN'T MUCH IN THE WAY OF A CONVERSATIONALIST, ARE YA, AGENT VORHEES?
THIAMINE MONONITRATE, RIBOFLAVIN, FERROUS SULFATE, NIACIN, DISDIUM GUANYLATE
I GOT A WEIRD VIBE ABOUT THIS CASE.
YOU GOT YOUR PIECE READY?
SIG P226. SEMI-AUTOMATIC. DOUBLE-ACTION. 9MM CART-RIDGE
YOU EVEN KNOW HOW TO USE IT?
...
<SIGH.>
TERRIFIC.

LOOK IT THAT ←BADASS BEAN JUMP!
SPECIAL PUNCH YO' MOMMA BREW
TALL 1.25 MED. 2.00 WTF 4.00
DEATH-SPRESSO - 2.45
LATTE - 2.00 3.00 4.50
SCONES - 1.25
WELCOME TO THE JUMPING BEAN.
MAY I TAKE YOUR ORDER?
AGENTS VALENZANO AND VORHEES. *FDA*. SPECIAL CRIMES DIVISION.
GOT A COUPLE QUESTIONS FOR YA.
JAVA IS OUR GOD!
CRAZY!
TIPS!
SURE.
CAN I OFFER YOU A LATTE? ON THE HOUSE?
HE'LL HAVE ONE.

EITHER O' THESE GUYS LOOK FAMILIAR TO YOU?
UM, NO, CAN'T SAY THEY DO.
ARE THEY SUPPOSED TO?
MILK
MAYBE.
ONE OF 'EM GOT SHOT TRYIN' TA KNOCK OVER A JEWELRY STORE THE OTHER DAY.
OTHER ONE GOT SLOPPY AN' WRAPPED HISSELF 'ROUND A TELEPHONE POLE TRYIN' TO MAKE AWAY WITH A LAMBORGHINI OFF SOME CLASSIC CAR LOT.
GEE, THAT SOUNDS AWFUL--
--BUT WHAT DOES THAT HAVE TO DO WITH--
COPS FOUND A COFFEE CUP IN THE CAR OF THE ONE GUY.
OTHER GUY HAD A TRASH CAN FULL OF COFFEE CUPS BACK AT HIS PAD.
SUGAR
SLEEPLESS NIGHTS LATTE -$4.55
COPS FIGURED IT WAS FOOD RELATED, SO THEY BUMPED IT OVER TO US.
YEAH. WE THOUGHT SO.
HMM, THAT'S PECULIAR.
DOUBLY PECULIAR ALL THEM CUPS WAS FROM THE JUMPING BEAN, TOO.
ANOTHER FOUND OUTSIDE A BANK JOB WEEK OR SO BACK.
FRWOOSH
TIPS!
WELL, GOLLY...
I SURE WISH I COULD BE MORE HELP.

HERE YA GO, BUDDY.
ENJOY.
KILL YOUR PARTNER
SSSSIPPP
--COFFEE BEANS, WHOLE MILK, COCOA BUTTER, LACTOSE--
VERY HOT-STUPID!
--SOY LECITHIN, CINNAMON, CHICORY--
VERY HOT-STUPID
COFFEE!!!

SPLSSSS
SHOVE
FWAMM
FaPOW
THE CURIOUS CASE OF THE BLACK-HEARTED BARISTA AND THE LETHAL LATTES.
EXIT
KILL THEM BOTH
MM-HMM.
AND WHAT DID YOU *DO*, CAESAR--
--TO EXTRICATE YOURSELF FROM THIS *MOST* UNFORTUNATE SITUATION?
SSSIPP

"EXTRICATE?"
WHAT THE HELL YOU THINK I DID, BIG MAN?
I PUNCHED A LOT O' MOTHER FUCKERS IN THE FACE --WHILE THE BAD GUY GOT AWAY.
RUINED MY FAVORITE SUIT, TOO, GOD-DAMMIT.
TURNS OUT AGENT RAIN MAN CAN'T READ--
--OR WE MIGHT BE MOURNIN' A WHOLE HELL OF A LOT MORE THAN MY BEST SUIT.
THIS COFFEE, CAESAR...
I'M NOT GETTING A FULL READING... JUST FRAGMENTS AND GHOST IMAGES.
I'M AFRAID WE MIGHT HAVE A PROBLEM.
SPEAKIN' O' PROBLEMS.
DWEET DWEET DWEET
IT'S CHU CALLIN'.
AGAIN.
TAKE THE CALL, CAESAR.
HUH?
TALK TO HIM.
SEE WHAT HE KNOWS. WHAT HE SUSPECTS.
GO AHEAD.
OLIVE WILL NOT BE A PROB-LEM.
H'LO?
MMMFF!
CAESAR!!

HEYA, TONY.
SORRY I AIN'T GOT BACK TO YOU, MAN.
.APPLEBEE BEEN RUNNIN' MY ASS RAGGED SINCE YOU AND COLBY GOT THE BOOT.
IT'S OKAY, CAESAR.
DON'T KNOW IF YOU HEARD MY MESSAGES--
--BUT MY DAUGHTER *OLIVE* HASN'T BEEN HOME FOR A WHILE, AND I--
SCREEE
TONY?
(HOLD ON A MINUTE, CAESAR.)
HEY, YOU'RE PARKING IN FRONT OF A FIRE HYDRANT.
IN *FRONT* OF A PARKING ENFORCEMENT OFFICER.
YOU *CAN'T* PARK THERE.
THAT'S ALRIGHT. WE AIN'T STAYIN'.
HEY-- DON'T I *KNOW* YOU?
YEAH, AS A MATTER OF FACT.
CRACK
CLICK
HUH?

WHAT IS IT, CAESAR?
I'M, UH, NOT SURE.
HEARD SOME FUNNY NOISES... THEN HE HUNG UP ON ME.
LOOK, ABOUT THE COFFEE--
I'LL NEED MORE TIME, CAESAR, AND IDEALLY A FEW MORE CUPS.
AS I SAID, WHAT FEW IMAGES I'M FLASHING UPON ARE WOEFULLY INCOMPL--
GIVE IT TO ME.
GIVE.
THE COFFEE.
TO ME.
GIVE IT TO HER, CAESAR.
LET HER DRINK IT.
NO.
NOT DRINK IT.
SNFFFFF

IT'S THE *BARISTA*.
YEAH, I *KNOW*, BUT HE'S BEEN USING A FAKE IDENTITY--
--AND WE AIN'T BEEN ABLE TO TRAC--
I *WASN'T* FINISHED.
HE'S AN *EFFERVIN-DUCTOR*.
THAT'S WHY *YOU* COULDN'T GET A READING. ALL THE *FOAM* IN THE LATTE HAD *DISSIPATED*.
I CAN GIVE HIS NAME. *I* CAN LEAD YOU TO HIM.
GIVE YOU *WHATEVER* YOU NEED.
BUT *NOT* IF YOU KEEP ME TIED UP. TRY TO FEED ME LIKE I'M SOME KIND OF TRAINED MONKEY.
TRY TO ORDER ME AROUND LIKE I'M SOME GOD-DAMN *LITTLE KID*.
YOU WANT TO *TRAIN* ME, *FINE*. BUT IT'S GONNA BE ON *MY* TERMS.
MY WAY.
I'LL BE YOUR *PARTNER*, BUT YOU ARE *NOT* GOING TO BE MY BOSS.
SO...
...DO WE HAVE A *DEAL*?

AND SO, A FEW HOURS LATER.
C'MON, SHITBAG. MOVE IT.
DO NOT CROSS
CRUNK
EASY THERE, PAL.
WATCH YER HEAD.
NICE WORK, AGENT VALENZANO.
FDA
YES, MY DEAR.
NICE WORK *INDEED*.

TONY CHU HAS BEEN KIDNAPPED.

HE WAS AMBUSHED, KNOCKED OUT, BROUGHT TO A REMOTE LOCATION, AND BOUND SECURELY.

HIS CAPTOR INTENDS TO *FEED* HIM FROM A MENU OF *HIS* CHOOSING, TO FIND OUT WHAT TONY CAN SEE, IN ORDER TO *LEARN* FROM HIM.

HERO!
HOME RUN!
PITCHER KILLED
--YOU'RE GOING TO.
END MAJOR LEAGUE CHEW: CHAPTER II

Chapter 3

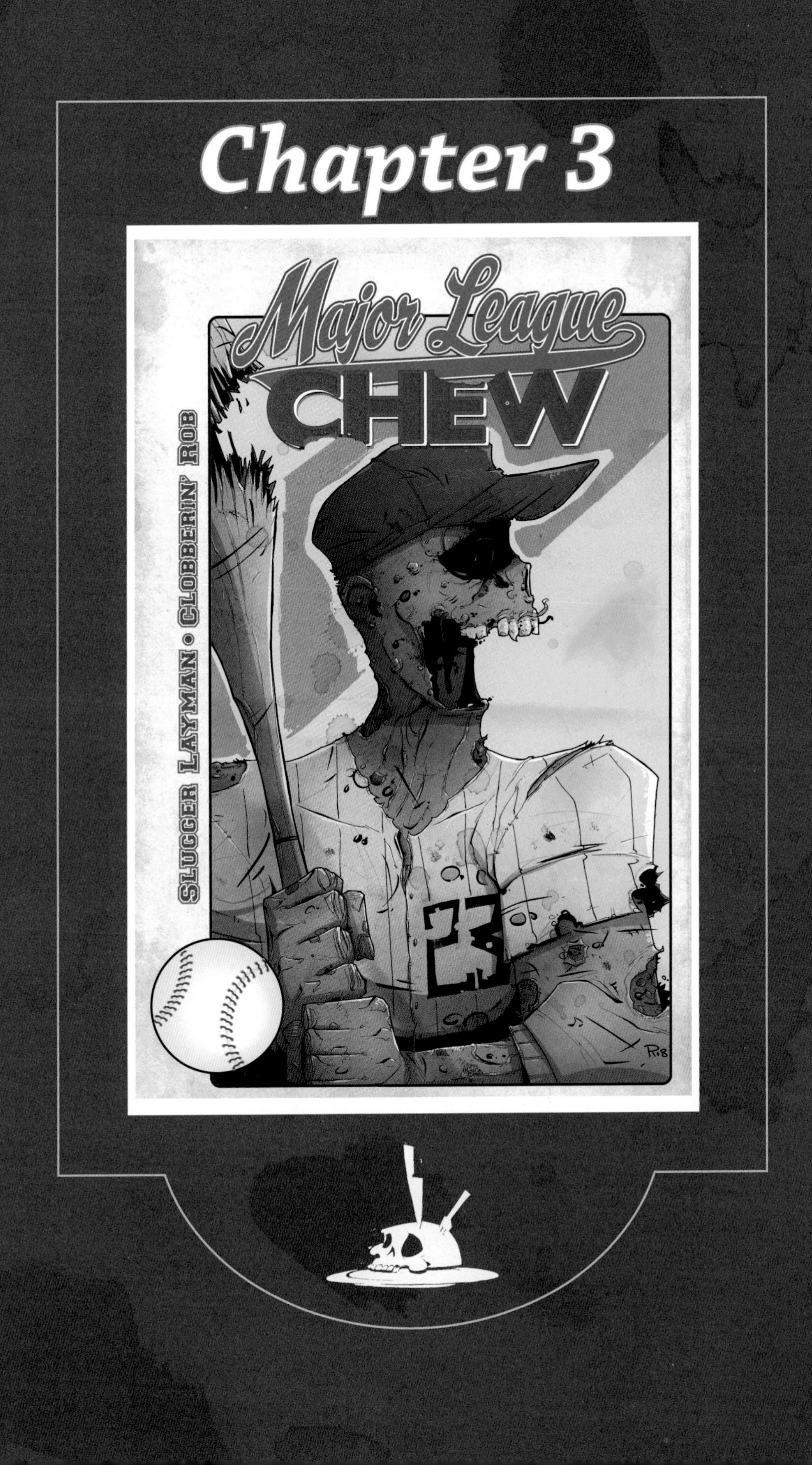

Major League
CHEW
SLUGGER LAYMAN • CLOBBERIN' ROB
23

USDA
USDA MEMO
SPINAL INSURANCE POLICY.
BY POPULAR DEMAND
USDA
USDA
THIS *ISN'T* WORKING OUT.
LITTERMEISTER 4000!
CLEAN UP AFTER YOUR PARTNER!

C'MON, TONY, PICK UP, YOU PRICK.
CLICK
THIS IS TONY! I'M UNAVAILABLE TO COME TO THE PHONE SO PLEASE LEAVE A MESSAGE AT THE BEEP--
AW, SONUVA...
BEEEEEEP
WHERE THE HELL *ARE* YOU, TONY?
AMELIA HASN'T HEARD FROM YOU EITHER. IS THIS JUST BECAUSE YOU'RE PISSED YOU GOT BOOTED OVER TO TRAFFIC DIVISION?
TONI SAYS YOUR HALF-PINT FLEW THE COOP, TOO. WHAT'S UP WITH THAT?
MAN, I'M TELLIN' YA, I GOTTA *DO* SOMETHING, TON.
THIS FUCKING *USDA* GIG SUCKS ENORMOUS SYPHILITIC MONKEY BALLS.
IN FACT, I SHOULD PROBABLY COUNT MY LUCKY STARS I DIDN'T GET *PARTNERED* WITH--
AGENT COLBY!
YOU'RE NOT USING A *USDA* PHONE FOR *PERSONAL* CALLS, *ARE* YOU?
BOOBIES ARE GREAT!
USDA
Chu, T.

OH, GOOD AFTERNOON, DIRECTOR PEÑYA.
NICE TO SEE YOU. I'VE BEEN MEANING TO TALK TO YOU.
I DON'T WANT TO HEAR IT.
THIS... BEAST YOU'VE GOT ME PARTNERED WITH.
WE'RE NOT REALLY CLICKING.
I REALLY NEED A NEW PARTNER.
I DON'T WANT TO HEAR IT.
LOVE THY ANIMAL
AGENT COLBY, I'M ON TO YOU. YOUR PREVIOUS DIRECTOR LEFT COPIOUS NOTES ON YOUR MANY FAULTS AND FAILINGS.
FAULTS? ME?!? APPLEBEE SAID I HAVE FAULTS?
I WAS WARNED, AGENT COLBY. YOU'RE A SLACKER AND A SHIRKER.
AN EXCUSE MAKER, AND A LOUSY EXCUSE FOR AN AGENT.
AND NOW I'M WARNING YOU:
DON'T.
THUMP
PISS.
ME.
OFF.
THIS SUCKS.

SPLURCH
WE HATE YOU, COLBY. —THE USDA.
USDA
OH, MAN.
THIS SUCKS WORSE THAN ANYTHING.
C'MON, TONY, PICK UP.
GEEZ, TONY, WHERE THE HELL ARE YOU?
I SWEAR, I'M HAVING THE WORST DAY.
ELSEWHERE:
LUNCH-TIME, MOTHER FUCKER.

YEAH.
TELL ME ABOUT THAT.

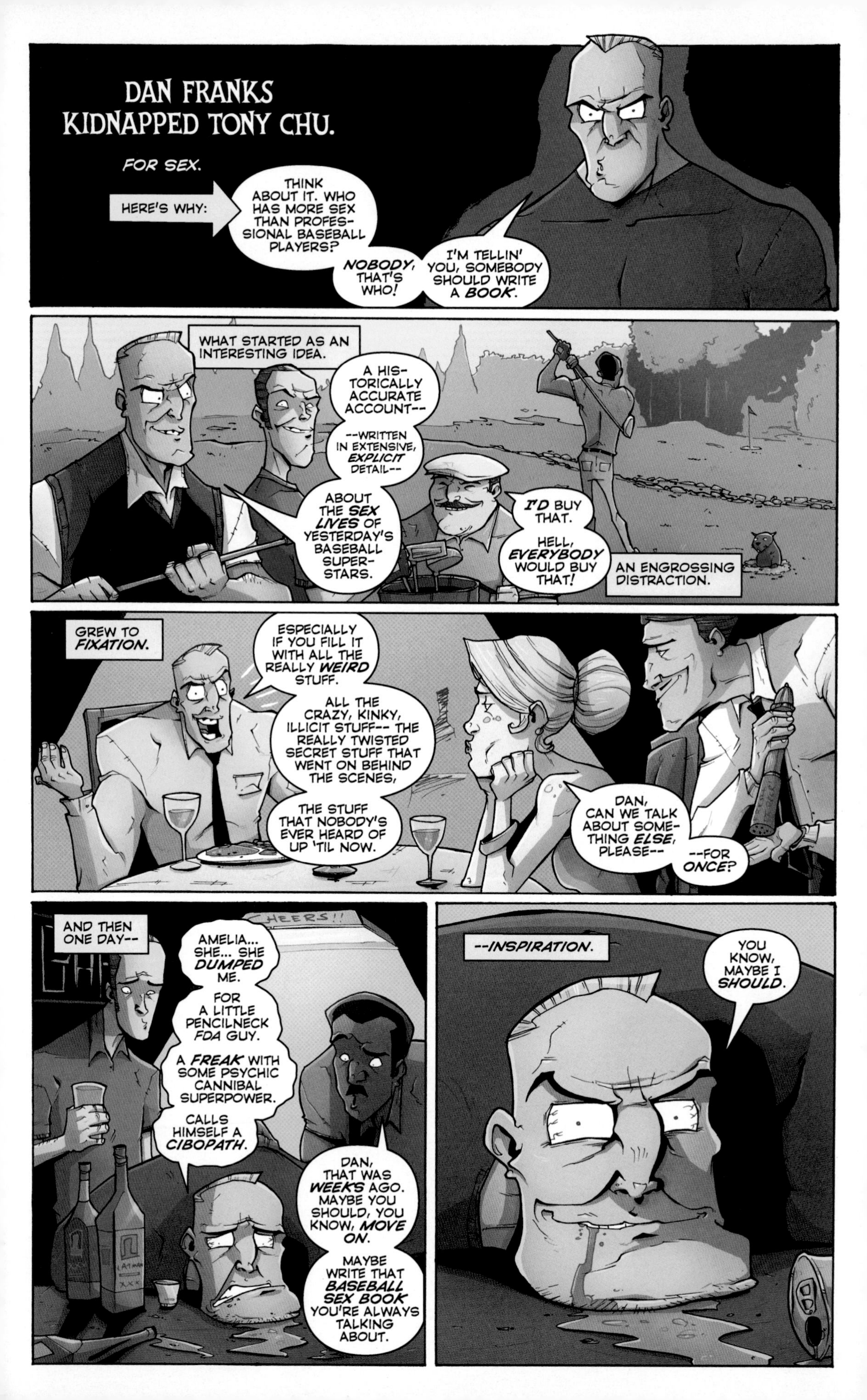
DAN FRANKS KIDNAPPED TONY CHU.
FOR SEX.
HERE'S WHY:
THINK ABOUT IT. WHO HAS MORE SEX THAN PROFESSIONAL BASEBALL PLAYERS?
NOBODY, THAT'S WHO!
I'M TELLIN' YOU, SOMEBODY SHOULD WRITE A BOOK.
WHAT STARTED AS AN INTERESTING IDEA.
A HISTORICALLY ACCURATE ACCOUNT--
--WRITTEN IN EXTENSIVE, EXPLICIT DETAIL--
ABOUT THE SEX LIVES OF YESTERDAY'S BASEBALL SUPERSTARS.
I'D BUY THAT.
HELL, EVERYBODY WOULD BUY THAT!
AN ENGROSSING DISTRACTION.
GREW TO FIXATION.
ESPECIALLY IF YOU FILL IT WITH ALL THE REALLY WEIRD STUFF.
ALL THE CRAZY, KINKY, ILLICIT STUFF-- THE REALLY TWISTED SECRET STUFF THAT WENT ON BEHIND THE SCENES,
THE STUFF THAT NOBODY'S EVER HEARD OF UP 'TIL NOW.
DAN, CAN WE TALK ABOUT SOMETHING ELSE, PLEASE--
--FOR ONCE?
AND THEN ONE DAY--
AMELIA... SHE... SHE DUMPED ME.
FOR A LITTLE PENCILNECK FDA GUY.
A FREAK WITH SOME PSYCHIC CANNIBAL SUPERPOWER.
CALLS HIMSELF A CIBOPATH.
DAN, THAT WAS WEEKS AGO. MAYBE YOU SHOULD, YOU KNOW, MOVE ON.
MAYBE WRITE THAT BASEBALL SEX BOOK YOU'RE ALWAYS TALKING ABOUT.
--INSPIRATION.
YOU KNOW, MAYBE I SHOULD.

AND THAT LED US *HERE*.
TELL YOU ABOUT *WHAT*? THE GIRLS?
YEAH! *EXACTLY!*
NOTES
WHAT THE HELL IS *WRONG* WITH YOU?
SCANDAL!
PITCHER SAYS: "THAT AINT MY KID!"
STAR?
SKPOW
FWAM
CRACK
KaWHAMM

YOU *LIKE* THAT, CHU?
'CAUSE I GOT *PLENTY* MORE. *HEAPS*.
AND IF YOU DON'T COOPER-ATE
BRINNNG BRRINNGGG
COLBY, J.
FONY
WILT C. CENTER
STATS: 1000 FEMAUD
KAWHAM!
THAT'S WHAT'S GONNA HAPPEN TO *YOU*.

GOD-DAMMNIT, TONY.
AGENT COLBY!
USDA
DO I REALLY NEED TO TELL YOU *AGAIN*?
SHIT PILE
FUMP
GET TO WORK.
WORK:
KOPY KAT
WE ♡ COPIES!! WAY TOO MUCH!!
COPIES- 5¢ !!
OPEN

MAKE COPIES!
THINGS ARE BETTER IN TWOS!
AGENTS COLBY AND BUTTERCUP. USDA. SPECIAL CRIMES DIVISION.
INK
SHIP TO:
PAPER
45¢ COLOR COPIES!!
MAY I HELP YOU?
GOT A FEELING YOU CAN, SPORT.
YOU, UH, NEED COPIES OF SOMETHING?
NOT EXACTLY.
HOPING YOU CAN MAKE CHANGE.
USDA
THINK YOU CAN BREAK A HUNDRED?
100
E PLURBUS MOOLAH.
BLING! BLING!

4815162342
4815162342
4815162342
FUNNY THING ABOUT *THIS* BILL.
TURNED UP IN AN ELECTRONICS STORE A FEW DAYS BACK.
ALONG WITH *FOUR* OTHERS WITH THE *EXACT* SAME SERIAL NUMBER.
IN FACT, STORES *ALL* OVER THE NEIGHBORHOOD ARE REPORTING BIG CASH PURCHASES-- AND THE *SAME BILL*.
THING IS, COPS HAVE BEEN HAVING A HARD TIME FOLLOWING THE EVIDENCE--
--MOSTLY BECAUSE THEY'RE HAVING A HARD TIME KEEPING THE *EVIDENCE*.
'COZ AFTER A WEEK OR SO THE BILLS START TO *DECOMPOSE*--
--AND A DAY OR SO LATER, THERE'S HARDLY ANYTHING LEFT.
USDA
THAT'S WHY IT GOT BUMPED OVER TO THE *UDSA*.
VEGETABLE BASED COUNTERFEITING.
PERFECT FORGERIES. LIMITED LIFESPAN.
CRONCH!
PROBABLY PRETTY GOOD WITH GARLIC SALT AND RANCH DIP, TOO.

SO ANYWAY, WHILE I WAS LOOKING INTO ALL THIS--
--I CROSSED-CHECKED RECENT BULK BUYS OF LOCAL PRODUCE WHOLE-SALERS--
SHIP TO: KOPYKAT
--AND NOTICED SOMETHING CURIOUS.
KITTY!
SNFF SNFF
NAMELY: WHY'S A KOPY KAT PRINTING JOINT BUYING A QUARTER TON OF YAMS EVERY THREE WEEKS?
GRRRRR
SHIP TO: KOPYKAT
NOW, I KNOW WHAT YOU'RE THINKIN', HOTSHOT--
WE LOVE COPIES
USDA
AN' LET ME TELL YA--
Plea No As on o Copie

YOU REALLY DON'T WANT TO DO ANYTHING STUPID.
GRRRRWWL
LATER:
USDA
NOT A BAD DAY'S WORK, EH, BUTTER-CUP?
NO BLOOD-SHED. NO GUN-PLAY. NOT EVEN AN EXCESSIVE FORCE COMPLAINT.
THAT'S GOTTA BE SOME KINDA RECORD.
USDA
YOU AND ME... WE DID ALL RIGHT TOGETHER.
WE PUT DOWN A FEW MORE CASES LIKE THESE, AND MAYBE THAT OLD HAG PEÑYA WILL FINALLY CUT ME SOME SLACK.
YAWN.

USDA
AND LATER STILL...
USDA
AGENT BUTTERCUP
THAT WAS SOME FINE WORK TODAY APPREHENDING THAT COUNTER-FEITING RING.
Skrtch scrtch
PURRR
ER, DIRECTOR PEÑYA...
...YOU KNOW, I WAS ACTUALLY THE PRIMARY ON THAT CASE.
AGENT COLBY--
THE BUST ITSELF WAS A JOINT EFFORT--
--BUT IT WAS MY DETECTIVE WORK THAT TRACKED THE COUNTER--
AGENT COLBY--
DA

IF YOU'RE TRYING TO IMPRESS ME, YOU'RE FAILING SPECTACU-LARLY.
FIND ANOTHER WAY.
YOU'RE NOT GOING TO GO FAR IN THIS DEPARTMENT IF THE BEST YOU CAN DO IS ATTEMPT TO STEAL CREDIT FOR ANOTHER AGENT'S COLLAR.
THIS PAPERWORK. MY DESK.
FIRST THING IN THE MORN-ING.
FUMP
NO EXCUSES, AGENT COLBY.
...
@#&%
HIP HIP HOORAY!
HIP HIP HOORAY!
I GOTTA GET OUT OF THIS BULLSHIT ASSIGN-MENT.
I'M NOT SURE HOW MUCH MORE I CAN TAKE.
TONY!? WHERE THE HELL ARE YOU, MAN?
YOU.

TONY CHU WAS KIDNAPPED.
FOR SEX!
HERE'S WHY:
TONY CHU IS *CIBOPATHIC*.
THAT MEANS HE CAN TAKE A BITE OF A PEACH AND GET A FEELING IN HIS HEAD ABOUT WHAT ORCHARD IT GREW AT, WHAT PESTICIDES WERE USED ON THE CROP, AND WHEN IT WAS HARVESTED.
OR HE CAN CONSUME THE RECENTLY EXHUMED CORPSES OF LONG-DEAD BASEBALL PLAYERS--
HERO!
--AND RECOUNT THE MOST SALACIOUS DETAILS OF THEIR *LOVE LIVES*.
AT LEAST *PRETEND* TO, ANYWAY.
--RED LACE UNDERWEAR, A BUS-LOAD OF NUNS, SPANISH FLY, AND TWO GALLONS OF CHOCOLATE PUDDING--
REALLY?!
LIAR!
LONG ENOUGH TO FORMULATE A *PLAN*.
THE *ENTIRE* VEGAS CHORUS LINE? IN THE *DUGOUT*? WITH A MARIACHI BAND?
AH, BUT THEN THINGS GOT *REALLY* WEIRD!
LIAR!

BASEBALL PLAYER BALLS SMASHED BY MISTRESS.
LONG ENOUGH TO FIND OUT WHAT HE NEEDED.
--LIKED TO CROSS DRESS AND BE BEATEN UP.
LOVED TO BE TIED UP AND WHIPPED.
DUDE LIKES BEING SPANKED BY SKILLET.
Scribble Scribble
IN ACTUALITY: EXPERT IN KNOTS.
BENEDICT BRADLEY
BROOKLYN DODGERS
'37-'44
PLAYER
--WAS INTO TWINS AND ONLY TWINS.
SOMETIMES, AFTER A BIG WIN, TWO OR THREE SETS OF THEM.
HE LIKED HORSES. (TOO MUCH.)
Scribble Scribble
IN ACTUALITY: DOUBLE JOINTED.
GRAVY JOHNSON
AMERICAN NEGRO LEAGUE
'29
BASEBALL PLAYER BALLS SMASHED BY MISTRESS.
--HAD A FETISH FOR CIRCUS PERFORMERS.
USED TO FOLLOW TRAVELING CIRCUSES AND SLEEP WITH THE ENTIRE FREAK SHOW.*
*AND THE CONTORTIONIST.
*AND THE ESCAPE ARIST.
Scribble Scribble
IN ACTUALITY: TRUE!
HAMISH O'BRIEN
WASHINGTON SENATORS
'54-'59
FUMP

ZZZZZZZZ
ZZZZZZZ
LOSING IS NOT AN OPTION. -LOMBARDI
I F*CKED YOUR MOMMA. -WILT.
ZZZZZZZZ
ZZZZZZ

HEY!
KRACK
WHERE THE FUCK YOU THINK YOU'RE GOING?

WHILE ELSEWHERE...
ZZZZZZZZ
LITTLE WOMEN
RIPPLE
END MAJOR LEAGUE CHEW: CHAPTER III
GRANNY PANTY.

Chapter 4

UNSALTED BUTTER!

NINETEEN MONTHS AGO:
THE TAJ MAHAL.
IN BUTTER!
IMPRESSIVE.
THE HMS BUTTERFORE.
NICE TECH-NIQUE.
MOUNT BUTTERMORE.
GOOD WORK.
BUTTERZILLA!
BUTTER AND BEHEMOTHS!
ANOTHER WORTHY ENTRY.

BOOTH
11
ASTONISHING.
MIND-BLOWING.
AMAZING.
ENTRY
14-J
INTER
BUTTER
SCULPTING
CHAMPI
SHIP!!!
BUT...
BUT...
IT'S CHOCO-LATE.
JUDGE #1

MR. BROWN... YOUR COMPETITION SUBMISSION...
IT'S INCREDIBLE... PHENOMENAL.
WARNING! FLOORS ARE BUTTERY!!
INTERNATIONAL BUTTER SCULPTING CHAMPIONSHIP!!!
12
OF COURSE IT IS. I WORKED ON IT FOR EIGHT STRAIGHT MONTHS--
--WITH A SINGLE GOAL IN MIND:
PERFECTION.
BUT THE BYLAWS ARE CLEAR.
CRYSTAL CLEAR.
BUTTER BY-LAWS
I'M SORRY, MR. BROWN. BUT YOUR SCULPTURE IS CHOCOLATE.
WE HAVE NO CHOICE BUT TO DISQUALIFY YOU.
BUTTER BY-LAWS
WHAT?!?
WE APPRECIATE YOUR EFFORTS, BUT--
EIGHT MONTHS. NONSTOP. FOR THIS COMPETITION AND THIS COMPETITION ALONE.
EVERY LAST ELEMENT OF THIS ARMOR WAS METICULOUSLY CRAFTED.
AND THE SWORD IS FULLY FUNCTIONAL.
I'M SORRY, BUT THIS IS A BUTTER SCULPTING COMPETITION--
"FULLY FUNCTIONAL?"
BUT THERE'S BUTTER IN CHOCOLATE!

MR. BROWN, YOU ARE *MISSING* THE *POINT*.
NO, *YOU* ARE.
AND HERE IT *IS*.
NOW... GIMME THAT DAMN TROPHY!

LATER:
ON THE 8TH DAY..
BUTTER!!
SPONSORED BY PAULA DEEN, YA'LL!!
ANY IDEA WHAT HAPPENED HERE, BIG MAN?
INDEED I DO, AGENT VALENZANO.
HERSHEL BROWN IS AN *EXTRAORDINARILY* SORE LOSER.
21
END PROLOGUE.

NOW.
AT THE HOUSE OF
OLIVE CHU!!
YOU CAN'T SPEND EVERY NIGHT LOCKED IN YOUR ROOM!
POUND POUND POUND
JUST LIKE YOU CAN'T RUN OFF FOR DAYS ON END WITHOUT TELLING US YOUR WHERE-ABOUTS--
--AND NOT EXPECT THERE TO BE CONSE-QUENCES.
DO YOU HEAR ME, YOUNG LADY?
COME OUT AND GET YOUR DINNE--
I ALREADY ATE.
I'M DOING MY HOME-WORK.
KEEP OUT
ANYTHING ELSE, AUNT ROSEMARY?
NO, BUT--
GOOD.
SLAM!
KEEP OUT!!
SERIOUSLY, DUDE.
THAT MEANS YOU!!!
KEEP OUT!!
OOOOOOH.

OLIVE IS--??
OLIVE IS BEING OLIVE.
SHE'S EXACTLY LIKE HER FATHER.
YOU KNOW, I SHOULD SEND HER BACK TO LIVE WITH HER FATHER.
DID I TELL YOU I CALLED HIM LAST WEEK TO TELL HIM OLIVE WAS GONE--
--AND HE HASN'T EVEN BOTHERED TO CALL BACK AND ASK ABOUT HER?
AS IF MR. FANCY-PANTS FDA AGENT IS TOO BUSY TO LOOK AFTER HIS OWN FLESH AND BLOOD!
BREWSKI
WITH HOPS! (WHAT'RE HOPS?)
ELSEWHERE:
YOU GOT TWO CHOICES, CHU.
EAT MORE... OR GET BEAT MORE.
TO HELL WITH HIM.
TO HELL WITH THE BOTH OF THEM!
SLAM!

RIGHT ON TIME, GIRLIE.
DON'T CALL ME GIRLIE.
WHAT'S THE WORD, FAT MAN?
CHOCOLATE, MY DEAR OLIVE.
THE WORD IS CHOCO- LATE.

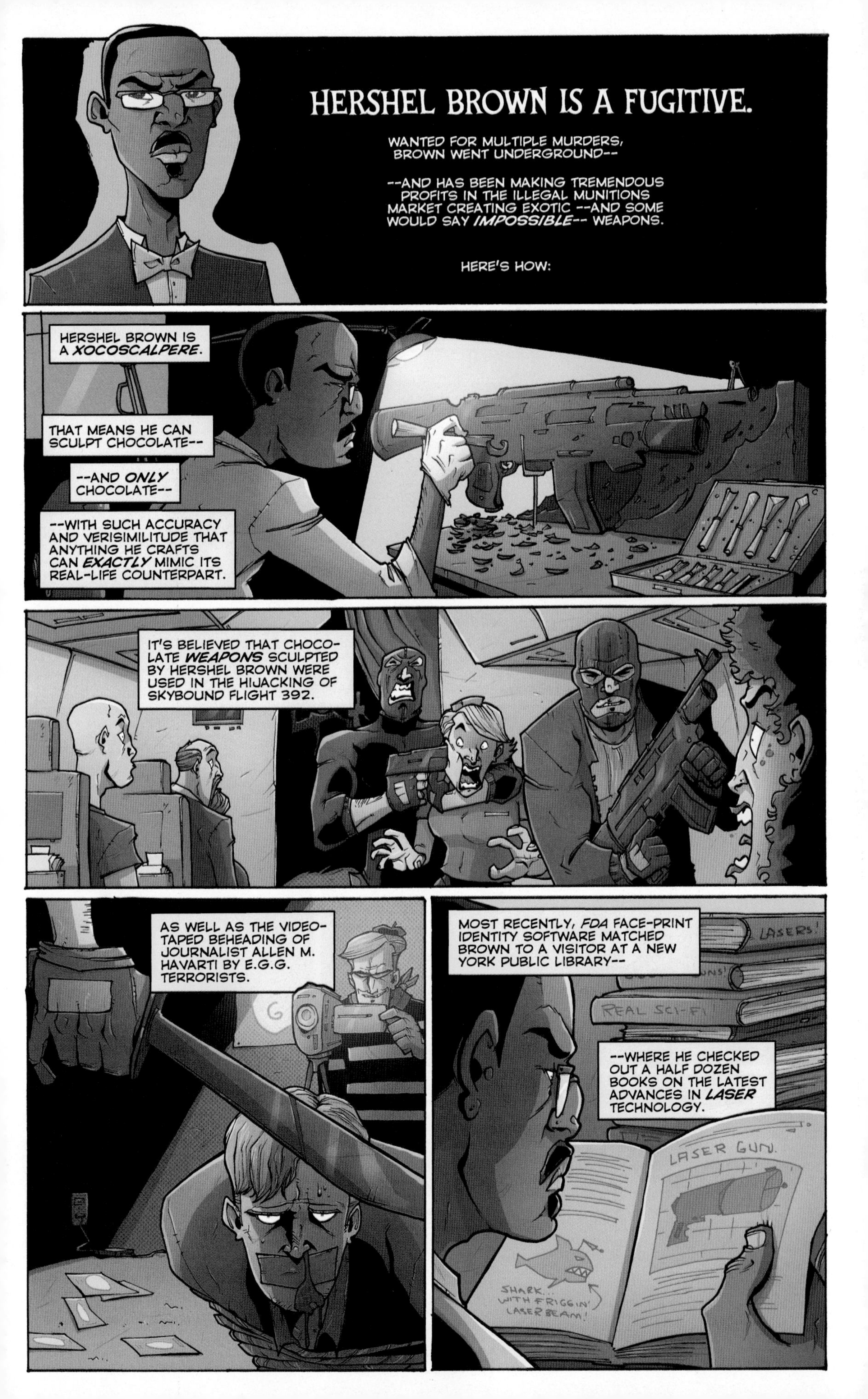
HERSHEL BROWN IS A FUGITIVE.
WANTED FOR MULTIPLE MURDERS, BROWN WENT UNDERGROUND--
--AND HAS BEEN MAKING TREMENDOUS PROFITS IN THE ILLEGAL MUNITIONS MARKET CREATING EXOTIC --AND SOME WOULD SAY *IMPOSSIBLE*-- WEAPONS.
HERE'S HOW:
HERSHEL BROWN IS A *XOCOSCALPERE*.
THAT MEANS HE CAN SCULPT CHOCOLATE--
--AND *ONLY* CHOCOLATE--
--WITH SUCH ACCURACY AND VERISIMILITUDE THAT ANYTHING HE CRAFTS CAN *EXACTLY* MIMIC ITS REAL-LIFE COUNTERPART.
IT'S BELIEVED THAT CHOCOLATE *WEAPONS* SCULPTED BY HERSHEL BROWN WERE USED IN THE HIJACKING OF SKYBOUND FLIGHT 392.
AS WELL AS THE VIDEOTAPED BEHEADING OF JOURNALIST ALLEN M. HAVARTI BY E.G.G. TERRORISTS.
MOST RECENTLY, *FDA* FACE-PRINT IDENTITY SOFTWARE MATCHED BROWN TO A VISITOR AT A NEW YORK PUBLIC LIBRARY--
LASERS!
REAL SCI-FI
--WHERE HE CHECKED OUT A HALF DOZEN BOOKS ON THE LATEST ADVANCES IN *LASER* TECHNOLOGY.
LASER GUN.
SHARK... WITH FRIGGIN' LASER BEAM!

HE'S MAKING CHOCOLATE LASER GUNS? ARE YOU FREAKING KIDDING ME?
CORRECTION: HE'S ALREADY MADE ONE.
AND NOW, HE'S TRYING TO SELL IT.
ME AND MY, UH, OTHER PARTNER.
WE GOT A WIRE-TAP UP ON BROWN.
OVERHEARD HIM IN DEEP NEGOTIATION, PLANNIN' A MEET FOR THIS VERY NIGHT.
SO, WHAT-- WE'RE GONNA STOP THE SALE AND BUST BROWN?
ER.
UH.
ACTUALLY, OLIVE, MY CHILD--
--IT'S A BIT MORE COMPLICATED THAN THAT.
WHICH LEADS US TO THIS.

I'D LIKE YOU TO TAKE A GOOD LONG SNIFF.
AND IF YOU WOULD BE AGREEABLE, PERHAPS A HEARTY TASTE AS WELL.
WHAT--
IT'S A CONCOCTION DESIGNED TO PREPARE YOU FOR THE CHALLENGE AHEAD.
THE NEXT PHASE OF YOUR TRAINING, SO TO SPEAK.
BUT FIRST, PERMIT ME TO ELABORATE:
YOU SEE, MY DEAR, AS YOU WILL SOON DISCOVER--
--THE PURSUIT OF THE TRUTH WE'VE CHOSEN TO ENGAGE IN WILL TAKE US DOWN SOME OF HUMANITY'S DARKEST PATHS...
...INTO BLACK RECESSES OF THE HUMAN HEART AND SOUL YOU'VE NOT ENCOUNTERED, PROBAB--
YEAH YEAH--IT'S CHOCOLATE, RIGHT?
YOINK!
SLURP
SPFFFFT

THAT'S BLOOD, FAT ASS.
YOU FUCKING MIXED BLOOD INTO A MILKSHAKE--
--AND TRIED TO FEED IT TO ME.
THREE HOURS EARLIER.
MERCY GENERAL ICU.
NURSE, I NEED THE CHARTS ON MR. CARROWAY, STAT!
W-WHAT'S GOING ON HERE?
WHO AUTHORIZED YOU TO TAKE A BLOOD SAMPLE?
DO YOU EVEN WORK HERE?
INDEED I DO NOT.
FWAM
NOW:
WHAT THE FUCK WERE YOU THINKING, ASSHOLE?
YOU DIDN'T GIVE ME A CHANCE TO EXPLAIN.
SAVE IT, BOTH OF YOU.
COL. Sanders Memorial Park
IT'S TIME.
WE'RE HERE.

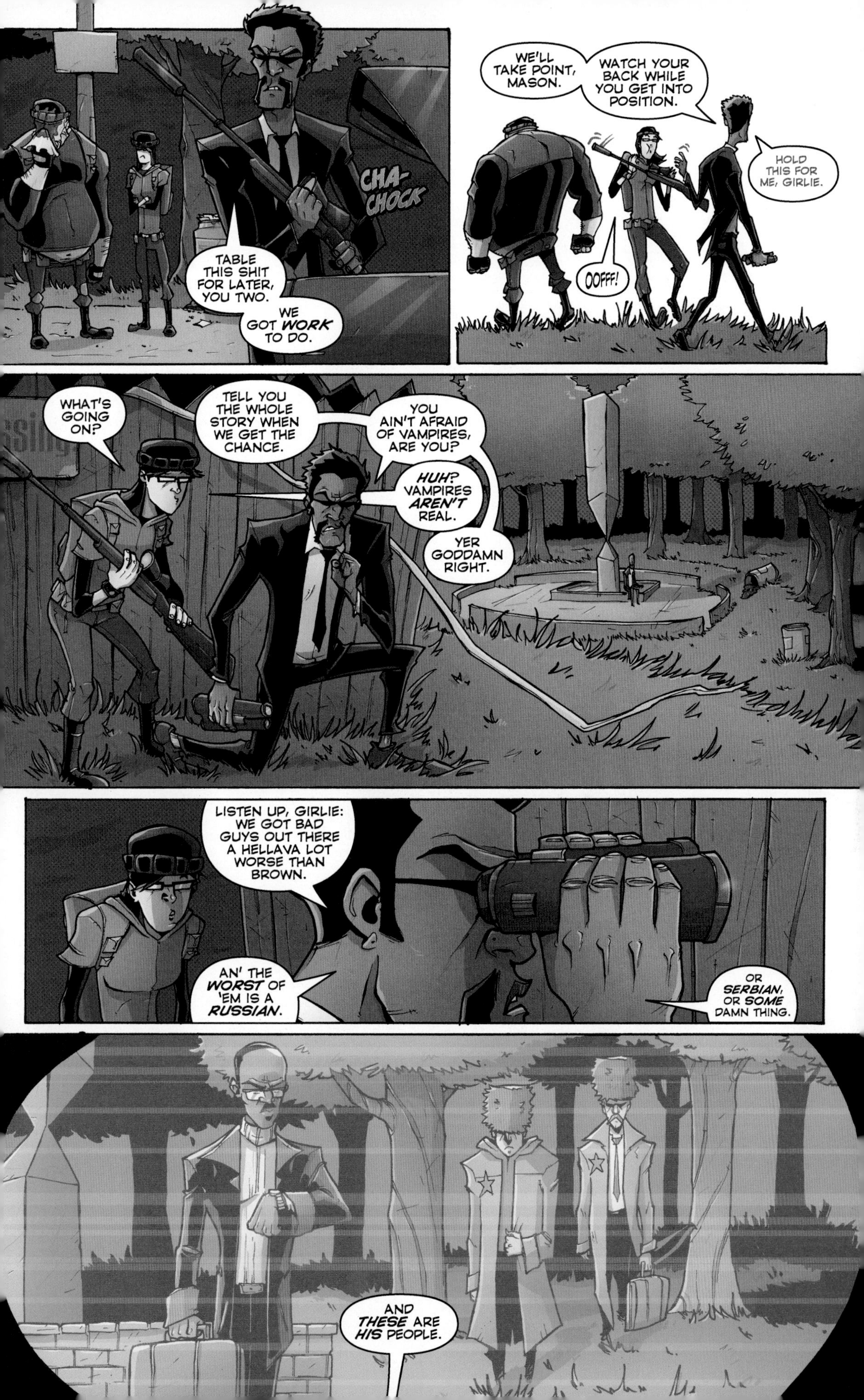
CHA-CHOCK
TABLE THIS SHIT FOR LATER, YOU TWO.
WE GOT WORK TO DO.
WE'LL TAKE POINT, MASON.
WATCH YOUR BACK WHILE YOU GET INTO POSITION.
HOLD THIS FOR ME, GIRLIE.
OOFFF!
WHAT'S GOING ON?
TELL YOU THE WHOLE STORY WHEN WE GET THE CHANCE.
YOU AIN'T AFRAID OF VAMPIRES, ARE YOU?
HUH? VAMPIRES AREN'T REAL.
YER GODDAMN RIGHT.
LISTEN UP, GIRLIE: WE GOT BAD GUYS OUT THERE A HELLAVA LOT WORSE THAN BROWN.
AN' THE WORST OF 'EM IS A RUSSIAN.
OR SERBIAN, OR SOME DAMN THING.
AND THESE ARE HIS PEOPLE.

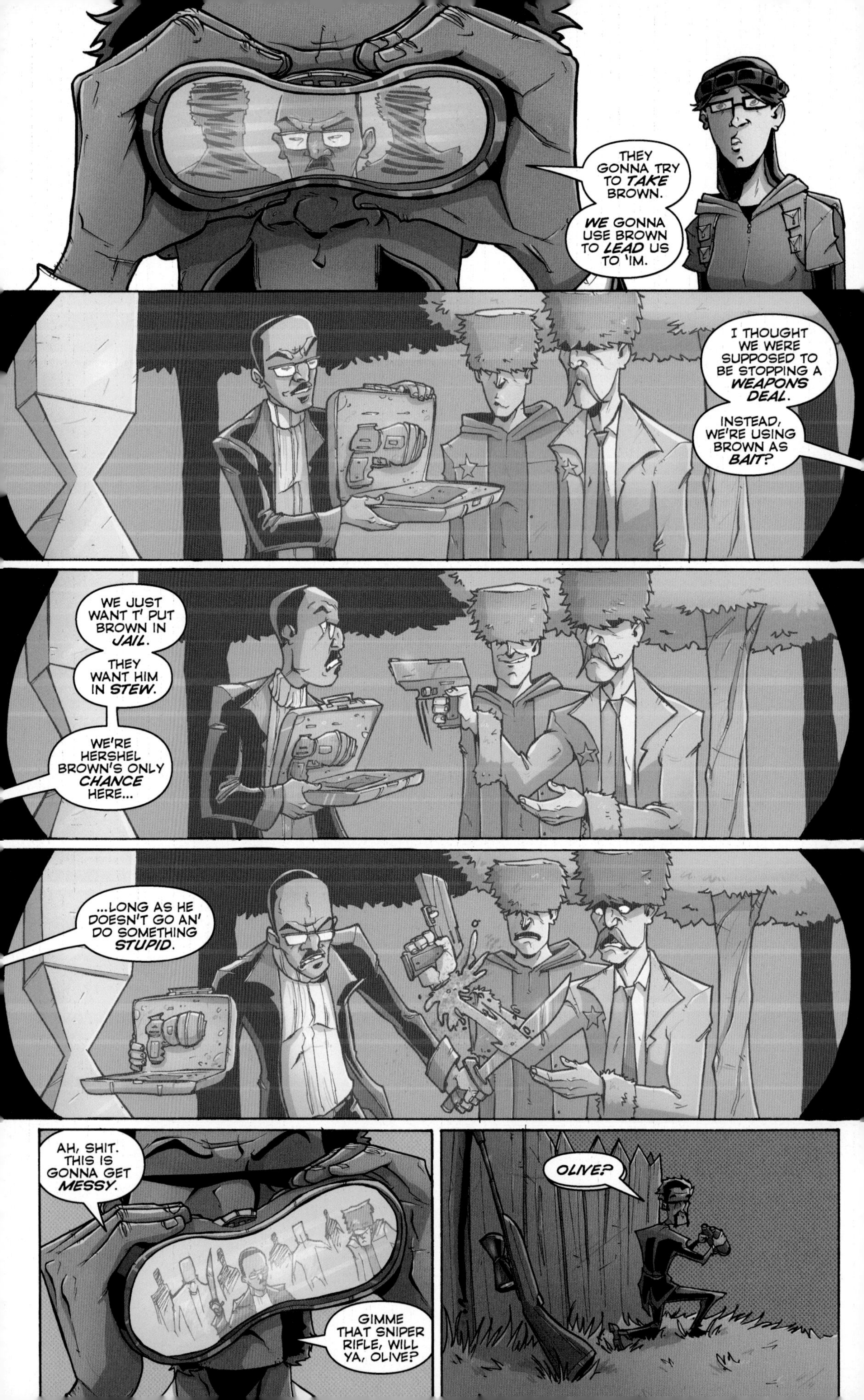
THEY GONNA TRY TO TAKE BROWN.
WE GONNA USE BROWN TO LEAD US TO 'IM.
I THOUGHT WE WERE SUPPOSED TO BE STOPPING A WEAPONS DEAL.
INSTEAD, WE'RE USING BROWN AS BAIT?
WE JUST WANT T' PUT BROWN IN JAIL.
THEY WANT HIM IN STEW.
WE'RE HERSHEL BROWN'S ONLY CHANCE HERE...
...LONG AS HE DOESN'T GO AN' DO SOMETHING STUPID.
AH, SHIT. THIS IS GONNA GET MESSY.
GIMME THAT SNIPER RIFLE, WILL YA, OLIVE?
OLIVE?

KRACK
KWAMM!!
SPLUT
BLAM
SKPOW

C'MON, I GOTTA GET YOU TO SAFETY.
WHO THE--
C'MON!
GRAB!
NO!
SHLK
FRZZZZT
FRZZZZZZZ

HOLY SHIT.
HOLY SHIT.
HOLY SHIT.
HOLY SH--
OLIVE, MY DEAR.
PERHAPS THIS IS NOT THE IDEAL TIME...
...BUT I NEED A MOMENT TO ELUCIDATE THE RATIONALE BEHIND MY EARLIER AND PERHAPS LAMENTABLE EPICUREAN ENDEAVOR.

WHA--?
THE MILK-SHAKE.
THREE WEEKS AGO THREE-TIME BLACK BELT WORLD KARATE CHAMP MATT CARROWAY WAS GRIEVOUSLY INJURED IN A MOTORCYCLE ACCIDENT.
HE'S BEEN IN INTENSIVE CARE EVER SINCE AND IS NOT EXPECTED TO SURVIVE.
THE BLOOD I PROCURED TO INCORPORATE INTO THE MILKSHAKE BELONGS TO HIM.
I DON'T UNDERST--
CIBOPATHS TAKE MORE THAN MEMORIES, IF THEY SO CHOOSE.
ABILITIES, AND KNOWLEDGE, THIS CAN BE ABSORBED AS WELL.
DEPENDING ON THE AMOUNT OF ORGANIC MATTER INGESTED, AND THE PARTICIPANT'S WILLINGNESS TO ABSORB.
I AM A CIBOPATH. YOUR FATHER IS A CIBOPATH-- THE MOST POWERFUL I'VE EVER MET-- AT LEAST UNTIL I MET YOU.
I BELIEVE YOU ARE SOME-THING MORE THAN A CIBOPATH, BUT EXACTLY WHAT I HAVE YET TO DETERMINE.
BUT I HAVE NO DOUBT THAT JUST THE SMALLEST EXPOSURE TO CARROWAY'S BLOOD ENHANCED YOUR REFLEXES TO THE POINT YOU WERE ABLE TO DODGE THAT LASER BARRAGE.
YOU'RE SAYING I CAN EAT--
I'M SAYING WHAT YOU CON-SUME, YOU CAN BECOME.
AND DIS-TASTEFUL AS IT MAY BE, YOU WILL FIND INSTANCES WHERE YOU WILL HAVE NO OTHER CHOICE.
AND THE, UH, RUSSIAN?
ANOTHER CIBOPATH.
AND A COLLECTOR OF OTHERS WITH EXTRAORDINARY TALENTS.
BUT IF IT'S ALL THE SAME TO YOU, I'D RATHER SAVE THAT CON-VERSATION FOR ANOTHER TI--
UH, BIG GUY?
FDA BACKUP EN ROUTE.
THINK YOU TWO BETTER CLEAR THE FUCK OUT OF HERE.
HMMM.

EPILOGUE.
SOME EVENING SHORTLY THEREAFTER, BACK AT THE HOME OF
OLIVE CHU!!
I WILL NOT HAVE YOU HOLED UP IN THAT ROOM FOR HOURS ON END.
COME OUT HERE THIS INSTANT AND EAT DINNER WITH THE REST OF US.
KEEP
POUND POUND POUND
NOW, MARCH OUT HERE THIS INSTAN--
DO YOU MIND, AUNT ROSEMARY?
I'M TRYING TO STUDY.
KEEP OUT!!
SERIOUS DUD
ALSO: I'M EATING IN MY ROOM.
I GOT SOME TAKE-OUT. ON MY WAY BACK FROM SCHOOL.
NOW...
...IF YOU'RE FINISHED INTERRUPTING MY EDUCATION--
KEEP OUT!!
SERIOUS DUD
MEANS YOU
SLAM!
KEEP OUT!!
OOOOOOH.

Snff Snff
PUBE-LIX MART
CHOMP
BLEGGGH
Scrip Scrape
CHOCO!
CHOCO!
Scrape Scrip Scrip
END MAJOR LEAGUE CHEW: CHAPTER IV

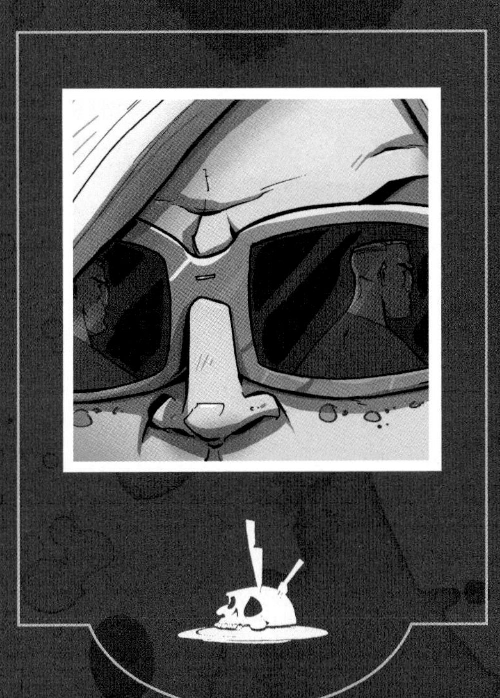

Chapter 5

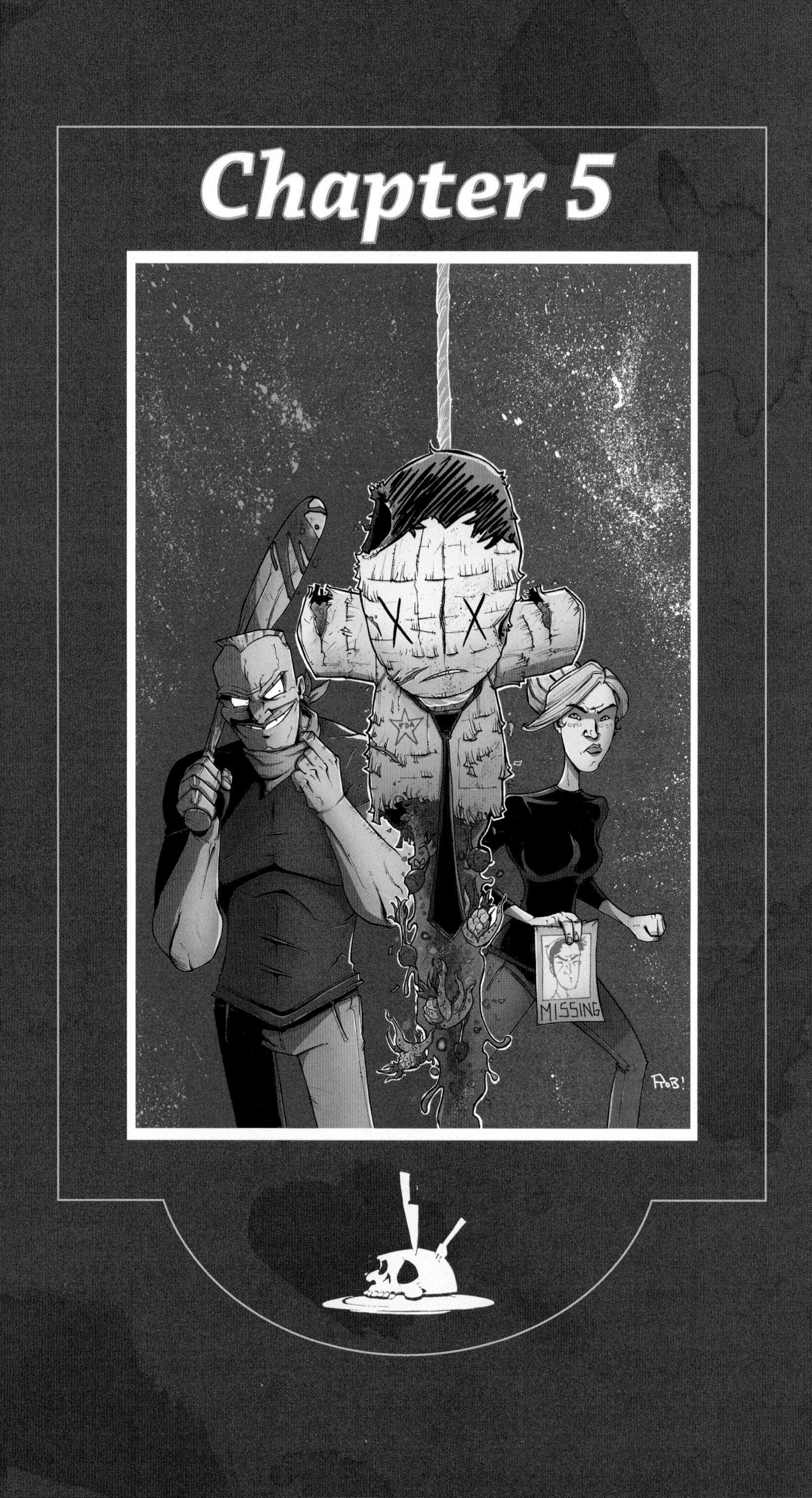

WHO'S IN THE MOOD FOR LOVE?
US

COME ON OVER HERE, BIG BOY.
POUR YOURSELF SOME BUBBLY, AND BUCKLE UP FOR ROUND TWO!
ER, DIRECTOR PEÑYA--
--I, UH, THOUGHT WE'D HAVE SOME TIME TONIGHT TO DISCUSS THE REQUEST I PUT IN FOR A NEW PARTNER.
OH, WE WILL, SUGAR-PLUM.
BUT FIRST, COME OVER HERE.
AND LET ME ROCK YOUR WORLD.

DWEET-
DWEET
DWEET
Caller: Amelia M.
BROWN BAGS PROVIDED BY HOTEL UPON REQUEST.
ER. I GOT A *PHONE CALL*, DIRECTOR PEÑYA.
I THINK I BETTER TAKE IT.
OH, IT CAN WAIT.
NO, I REALLY THINK--
AGENT COLBY, AS YOUR *COMMANDING OFFICER* AND YOUR *DIRECT SUPERIOR* I AM TELLING YOU--
--WHAT*EVER* IT IS--
--IT CAN *WAIT*.
Caller: Amelia M.
NOW, GET *OVER* HERE, YOU GORGEOUS HUNK OF CYBERNETICALLY-ENHANCED BEEFCAKE.
Caller: Amelia M.
DWEET
DWEET
DAMMIT.

MUNICIPA
TRAFFIC
HQ
"PLEASE DON'T HATE US. IT'S THE LAW."
I'M SORRY MS.--
MINTZ. AMELIA MINTZ.
KILT CLEANERS: PARK AT REAR.
ILLEGAL PARKING HERE WILL CAUSE VEHICLE IMPLOSION.
YES, SO SORRY, MS. MINTZ, BUT OFFICER CHU HASN'T REPORTED TO WORK IN SEVERAL DAYS.
I KNOW. HE HASN'T BEEN HOME EITHER.
LICENSE TO PARK.
THAT'S WHAT I'M TELLING YOU. THIS ISN'T NORMAL.
SOMETHING IS TERRIBLY WRONG.
MOTIVAT
IF THIS DOESN'T YOU HAPPY, KIL
WELL... ER... I'M SORRY, MS. MINTZ, BUT I'M NOT SO SURE.
WHAT DO YOU MEAN BY THAT?
I TALKED TO HIS FORMER SUPERIOR, HIS EX-BOSS AT THE FDA--
--AND HE SAID THIS SORT OF BEHAVIOR WAS PERFECTLY IN CHARACTER FOR ANTHONY CHU.
MIKE APPLEBEE SAID THAT?
MIKE APPLEBEE SAID THIS:
TONY CHU?
ONLY THE MOST MISERABLE, PATHETIC, INCOMPETENT, OFFENSIVE, ABRASIVE, UNPLEASANT, OBNOXIOUS AND ALTOGETHER OBJECTIONABLE EXCUSE FOR A LAW ENFORCEMENT OFFICER IT'S EVER BEEN MY EXTREME DISPLEASURE TO WORK WITH.
AND LET ME TELL YOU SOMETHING ELSE.
HE DID INDEED, MS. MINTZ. AND MANY OTHER THINGS.
TERRIBLE THINGS.

I'M SORRY, MS. MINTZ.
I DIDN'T WANT TO BELIEVE IT EITHER.
IN OUR BRIEF TIME TOGETHER, OFFICER CHU REALLY IMPRESSED ME.
BUT AFTER WHAT FDA DIRECTOR APPLEBEE TOLD ME, AND WHAT I READ IN CHU'S FILE--
WHAT?!?
WHATEVER WAS IN TONY'S FILE WAS PROBABLY WRITTEN BY APPLEBEE.
MIKE APPLEBEE HATES TONY'S GUTS.
HE'S ALWAYS HATED HIM, AND HE ALWAYS WILL HATE HIM.
ISSUE #60:
I STILL HATE YOU, CHU.
I'M SORRY, MS. MINTZ.
I SINCERELY HOPE I'M WRONG, AND I SINCERELY HOPE YOU ARE RIGHT.
I ALSO HOPE NO HARM HAS BEFALLEN DETECTIVE CHU.
BUT I'M AFRAID IT'S OUT OF MY HANDS.
ANTHONY CHU IS NO LONGER A MEMBER OF THE MUNICIPAL TRAFFIC ENFORCEMENT DIVISION.
DAMMIT.
WE HATE YOU!

OH, GOSH, AMELIA. ARE YOU SERIOUS?
TONY? MISSING?
THAT DOESN'T SOUND LIKE HIM AT ALL. I'D HELP YOU, BUT I'M SORTA ON ASSIGNMENT AT THE MOMENT.
NO, I HAVEN'T SEEN HIM.
I SWEAR, HE'S JUST LIKE THAT DAUGHTER OF HIS.
TONY?!? FUCK NO! GOOD RIDDANCE!
PHOTOS WITH CHOW $20!! (NO TOUCHING CHOW!!)
CHOW'S GOOD GRUB!
CHOW FAN CLUB!!
NAH, I AIN'T SEEN HIM.
NOT REALLY LIKE OL' STRAIGHTLACED TONY CHU TO TAKE OFF UNANNOUNCED THOUGH, IS IT?
DAMMIT.
PROPERTY OF: SUN
DON'T KICK COPIER, PLEASE!
SUN!

WHATS-AMATTER, 'MELIA?
MISS HAVING A REAL MAN AROUND?
OR ANY KIND OF MAN AROUND FOR THAT MATTER?
FRANKS, D. MY SHIT.
TPS REPORTS WTF?!!
PROPERTY OF SUN
SCREW YOU, DAN.
SORRY, BABE. YOU HAD YOUR CHANCE.
SEE YA.
WHERE'S HE GOING?
YOU HAVEN'T HEARD?
HE FINALLY GOT A DEAL ON THAT BOOK HE'S ALWAYS TALKIN' ABOUT.
NO JIBBA-JABBA HERE!
"SUPERSTAR SLUGGERS' UNTOLD SEX TALES?"
EWWW.
YEAH. MUST HAVE GOTTEN A BIG ADVANCE, BECAUSE HE WALKED IN--
--DROPPED HIS RESIGNATION LETTER ON MY DESK, AND LEFT WITH HIS STUFF.
DIDN'T EVEN HAVE THE DECENCY TO PUT IN TWO WEEKS.
NO BERETS!
SUN
AMELIA?
HOW DID DAN KNOW TONY HASN'T BEEN AROUND?

!!!
I GOTTA GO, HERB.
WHAT?!? YOU'RE ON DEADLINE. YOU GOT A STORY TO TURN IN.
I GOTTA GO.
DAMMIT, AMELIA, YOU'VE GOT WORK TO DO.
YOU WANT A STORY, RIGHT?
THIS IS WORK.
WORK:
DEROCHE, MAX
FARE: 0
FOLLOW THAT CAR.
ISLAND LIMOS INC.
DRIVE TO THE CRIME SCENE... IN STYLE!

OPEN!
DOWNTOWN THEATRE!
CLOSED
WHOA WHOA WHOA, LITTLE LADY.
YOU DON'T *LOOK* LIKE ONE OF THE ATTENDEES, SO IF YOU AIN'T GOT AN *INVITATION*, YOU *AIN'T* GETTIN' IN.
SPACE FOR RENT!
HEADBUTT
BRO
痴

INVITATION? EXACTLY WHAT'S GOING ON IN THERE?
LADY, I'M GETTIN' PAID GOOD MONEY *NOT* TO TALK ABOUT IT.
SO IF YOU *DON'T* KNOW, THAT'S BECAUSE YOU'RE NOT *SUPPOSED* TO.
NOW MOVE ALONG.
HEAD BUTT

INSIDE:
HELLO, HELLO!
YOU'RE *LATE*, DAN.

FASHIONABLY SO, I LIKE TO THINK. BUILD SOME ANTICIPATION, AND WE GET A BETTER *PRICE*.
HOW'S IT GOIN' IN THERE, ANYWAY?
EVERY-BODY'S GETTING ANTSY.
MARILYNS AND THE KINGS DON'T SEEM TO LIKE EACH OTHER MUCH.
TOSS UP BETWEEN WHO'S CREEPIER, SATANISTS OR THE NAZIS--
--AND THOSE DAMN CIVIL WAR REENACTORS WAVING THEIR MUSKETS AROUND AT EVERY-BODY--
THEY'RE NOT *LOADED*, ARE THEY?
HELL, THEY'RE NOT EVEN *REAL*.

YOU READY FOR THE BIG SHOW, DAN?
OH YEAH...
LET'S *DO* THIS THING.

HELLO.
MY NAME IS DAN FRANKS.
AND I HAD A DREAM.
A DREAM ABOUT BASE-BALL.
AND TO WRITE THE ULTIMATE TELL-ALL BOOK ABOUT THE SECRET, SORDID SEX LIVES--
--OF ALL THE BASE-BALL GREATS WHO'VE MADE OUR NATIONAL PASTIME SO RIVETING AND UNFORGETTABLE OVER THE YEARS.
THIS IS THAT BOOK.
SUPER STAR SLUGGERS UNTOLD SEX TALES
"SUPERSTAR SLUGGERS' UNTOLD SEX TALES."
$$$
AND THIS IS THE SEVEN-FIGURE CHECK I GOT FROM A MAJOR NATIONAL PUB-LISHER FOR THE RIGHTS TO PRINT MILLIONS OF COPIES OF MY BOOK.
YOU'RE HERE TODAY BECAUSE YOU HAVE A DREAM, TOO.
AND BECAUSE I'M OFFERING A CHANCE TO MAKE YOUR DREAM A REALITY.
WITH THE HELP OF CIBO-PATHY.
WHAT IS CIBO-PATHY?
WELL, IT'S THE ABILITY TO READ MEM-ORIES, TO SEE THE PAST, AND TO LEARN TRUTH--
--THROUGH EATING.
I'M ABOUT TO INTRODUCE YOU TO TONY CHU--
--THE CIBOPATH WHO HAS BEEN INSTRUMEN-TAL TO THE RESEARCH OF MY BOOK.
IT'S NO EXAGGERA-TION TO SAY THAT WITHOUT MR. CHU, AND HIS INVALUABLE ASSISTANCE--
--I COULD NEVER HAVE ACHIEVED MY DREAM, OR SOARED TO THE GREAT HEIGHTS I HAVE TODAY.
AND NOW, I OFFER YOU A CHANCE TO DO THE SAME.
THIS IS YOUR OPPOR-TUNITY.
AND IT WON'T COME ALONG AGAIN.
LET'S BEGIN.

HIGHEST BID:
$0
WHO'S GOING TO START THE *BIDDING*?
POP

GHEST BID:
$0
DID HAN SHOOT FIRST ?
EXIT
CORN
ILLINOIS DIVISION.

NOT LONG THEREAFTER.
HEAD BUTT
LITTLE WOMEN
SPACE FOR RENT!
SPACE FOR RENT! PLEASE! SMELLS JUST A BIT LIKE PEE!
FRUIT CUPS!!
SO, UH, HOW'S IT GOING IN THERE?
AH, HONEY, LET'S PUT IT THIS WAY:
WHAT HAPPENED IN MARILYN GON' STAY IN MARI-LYN.
WHAT?
THE AUCTION, OF COURSE.
WE LOST.
AUCTION?
MEMO.
Scribble Scribble Scribble
YOU THERE.
READ THIS.

AMELIA MINTZ IS
TONY CHU'S GIRLFRIEND.

SHE'S ALSO A *SABOSCRIVNER*.

CONGRATULATIONS.
I THINK YOUR, UH, LITTLE SCIENCE CLUB IS GOING TO BE *QUITE* HAPPY WITH YOUR PURCHASE.
WE'RE A *PRIVATELY* FUNDED *RESEARCH* FACILITY, MR. FRANKS AND, YES, WE'RE *VERY* EXCITED.
WE'VE GOT BIG PLANS TO EXHUME EINSTEIN, AND THEN SAGAN, TESLA, CURIE--
BALLZ
YOU CAN DITCH THE SMALL TALK, DORKS. ALL I REALLY CARE ABOUT IS YOUR *MONEY*.
DAN.
SNAP
HAND OVER MY BOYFRIEND.
RIGHT *NOW*, YOU SON OF A BITCH.
SHIT.
YOU GUYS: BRING BACK THOSE EGG-HEADS--
--AND GET OUR *MONEY*.
EXIT
I'LL TAKE CARE OF MY *EX*.

LET HIM GO, DAN, OR YOU'RE GONNA REGRET IT.
I KINDA DOUBT IT.
I'LL FUCKIN' HURT YOU, I SWEAR.
WITH A PLASTIC BAYONET?
GOOD LUCK WITH THAT.
WHILE I'VE GOT THIS GREAT BIG RAZOR-SHARP KNIFE.
AND A WHOLE LOT OF EMOTIONAL ISSUES TO WORK THROUGH.
MOST OF THEM ANGER ISSUES.
Y-YOU..
YOU'RE NOT GONNA TOUCH HER.
WHO'S GONNA STOP ME? YOU?!?
FUCK YES I AM.

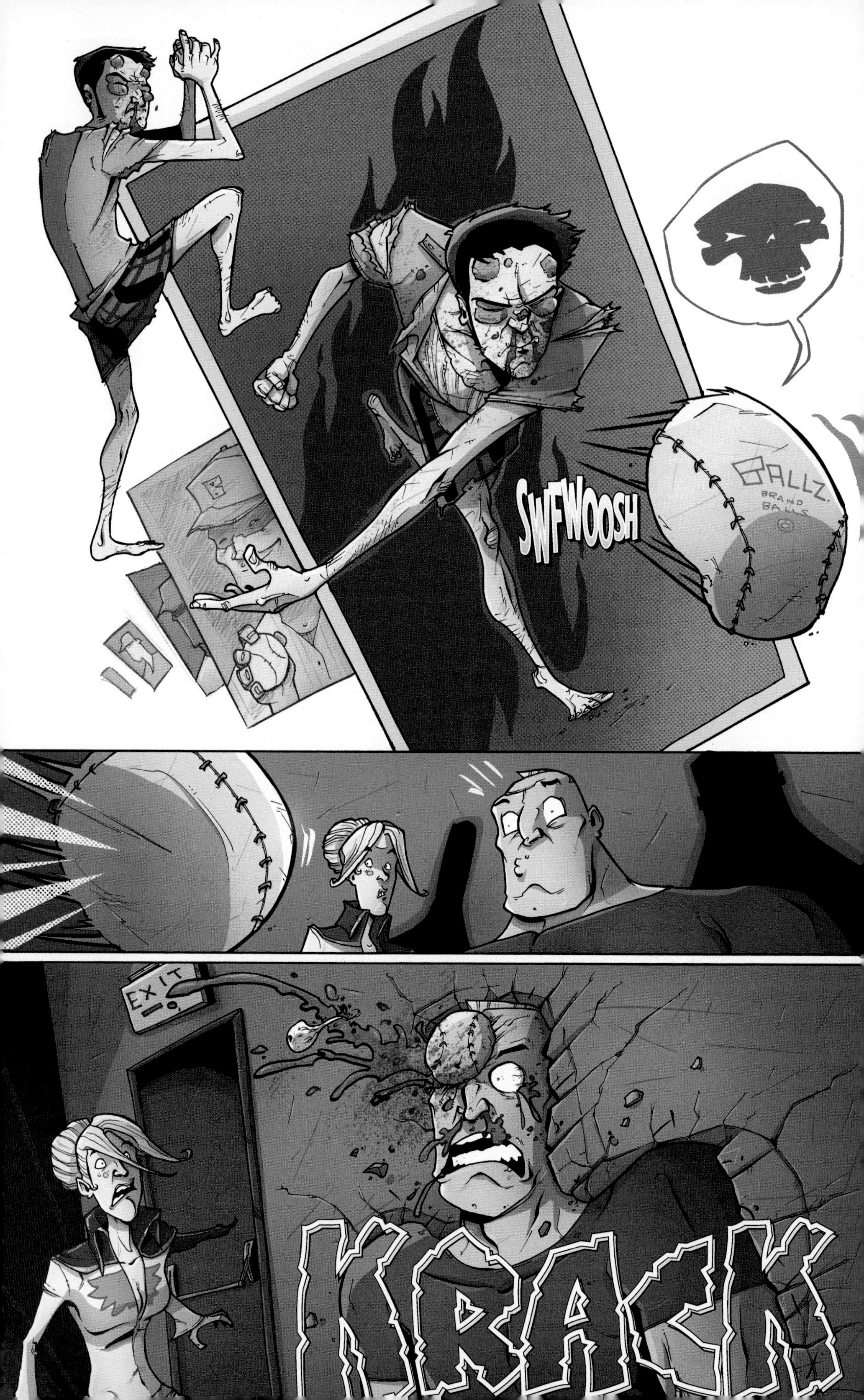
SWFWOOSH
BALLZ.
BRAND
BALLS
EXIT
KRACK

TONY!
FLUMP
T-THANKS FOR C-COMING FOR ME, 'MELIA.
I L-LOVE Y-YOU.
I LOVE YOU TOO, TONY.
HOW DID YOU DO THAT?
WH-WHEN DID YOU LEARN TO THROW A BASEBALL LIKE THAT?
ALL S-STAR GAME '62.
W-W-WORLD SERIES '54...
...AND '71.
TONY?
TONY?

EPILOGUE:
SOME TIME LATER.
BRRING BRRING
USDA, COLBY HERE. WHADDAYA WANT?
HI JOHN.
AMELIA! QUE PASA, CHICA?
I--I'VE GOT SOME BAD NEWS, JOHN...
...ABOUT TONY.
AGENT COLBY!
MY OFFICE.
NOW.
I NEED TO TAKE THIS CALL, DIRECTOR PEÑYA.
IT'S IMPORTANT.
NO, AGENT COLBY.
THIS IS IMPORTANT.
JOHN?
Caller: Amelia M.
WHAT--
I'VE GOT SOME GOOD NEWS, JOHN.
USDA

--ABOUT YOUR NEW PARTNER.
MY--?
YOUR REQUEST, AGENT COLBY.
IT'S APPROVED.
BASED ON YOUR <AHEM> EXEMPLARY RECENT JOB PERFORMANCE.
U.S.D.A.
EMPLOYEE OF THE MONTH!
REALLY!?!
I MEAN, THAT'S GREAT.
YOU KNOW, I HAVE SOME THOUGHTS ON THAT, DIRECTOR PEÑYA.
MY PREVIOUS PARTNER...
...WE WORK REALLY WELL TOGETHER...
ER, MAYBE HE COULD BE TRANSFERRED IN AND--
DENIED.
AGENT COLBY, YOU ARE BEING PARTNERED WITH THE USDA'S ABSOLUTE BEST AND BRIGHTEST.
OUR ONLY AGENT WITH A 100% MISSION SUCCESS RATE.
A STONE KILLER.
PURE LETHAL FORCE.

POYO!!!
NUT. FACTS.
FIBER 8%
STEEL 10%
IRON 5%
DOOM 95%
PROPERTY OF USDA
POYO.
END CHEW BOOK V: MAJOR LEAGUE CHEW.

The new Mecha-Poyo. I wanted the design to feel like a souped-up Hot Rod, complete with big honkin' exhaust pipes.

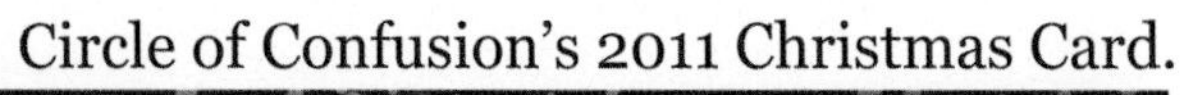

Circle of Confusion's 2011 Christmas Card.

The Script. Layouts are drawn directly on the page.

Issue #25
"Major League Chew"
(part 5 of 5)
by John Layman

PAGE ONE
FULL PAGE SPLASH
On USDA Director Peñya, looking brazen and seductive, looking directly at the audience with her best come-hither stare. There's a bed in the background, possibly heart-shaped, covered in rose petals. Penya is holding a bottle of just-opened champagne and two flutes. She is wearing some provocative lingerie. I suggest you check out Trashy.com for reference, which has spectacularly awesomely elaborate lingerie, equally overpriced. Anyway, she is wearing some elaborate outfit from there, some sort of bustier/corset thing, with fishnet stockings and kinky high-heeled boots. Of course, she's also old as hell, so she's got age-spots and sagging skin and of course her hunchback. In fact, maybe she's not holding the champagne bottle. It is just siting nearby, so she can be holding her cane. She's also wearing make-up, and not well. Overly wearing it.
Anyway, she looks old and horrific, and for as much as she is trying to seduce, it should have a ghoulish opposite effect—we're going for laffs here.
Be funny, maybe, if she had a USDA patch tattooed on her arm.

PENYA (hearts around balloon): Who's in the mood for love?
***

PAGE TWO
PANEL ONE
And now a different angle, to see she is addressing Colby, who is in his regular street close. We're playing Penya like an oversexed cougar –and over-aged by several decades. Colby thought he would work his charms on her, but it's backfired, and he's finding that Penya is insatiable, and won't take no for an answer. She is moving toward him, and Colby is backing award, trying to mask his horror.

PENYA: Come on over here, big boy.

PENYA: Pour yourself some bubbly, and buckle up for round two!

PENYA: Er, Director Peñya --

PENYA: --I thought we'd have some time tonight to discuss the request I put in for a new partner.

PANEL TWO
Angle from behind, and she is unclasping or undoing whatever she is wearing. Good angle of her hunchback. Ha!

PENYA: Oh, we will, sugarplum.

PANEL THREE
Pan down, just to see her feet, as whatever she was wearing drops to the ground. Behind her, Colby's eyes bulging out of his head, and not in a good way.

PENYA: But first, come over here.

PANEL FOUR
On the two of them, from the shoulders up as Penya moves toward a cornered against the wall Colby.

PENYA: And let me rock your world.
***

PAGE EIGHT
Three smallish panels followed by a big one that's half the page, like we did we a similar caption in #22 and #23.

PANEL ONE
On Amelia. A look of revelation. She just got the craziest idea that Dan might be up to something involving Tony—and she's right!!
--SILENT PANEL

PANEL TWO
She grabs here purse and stands up, look of urgency on her face. Her editor does not understand.

AMELIA: I gotta go, Herb.

HERB: What?!? You're on deadline. You got a story to turn in.

AMELIA: I gotta go.

PANEL THREE
Amelia heads quickly for the door, even over her editors protests.

HERB: Dammit, Amelia, you've got work to do.

AMELIA: This is work.

PANEL FOUR
Half the page. Amelia in the back of a cab, pointing to Dan's car pulling onto the city street just ahead of her, as Amelia directs the cabbie to follow him.

CAPTION: Work.

AMELIA: Follow that car.
***

PAGE NINE
PANEL ONE
A bit later, Amelia walking down the street, wearing big sunglasses, trailing from a distance, Dan up ahead, obviously he is being followed. Dan is cheerful, on his way to, and looking forward to, a big event.
--SILENT PANEL

PANEL TWO
Another panel like the last, but a different street, different angle
--SILENT PANEL

PANEL THREE
Over Amelia's shoulder, to see Dan entering some large unmarked building, (an old abandoned theater rented expressly for the auction, but that's not terribly important) getting past a pair of burly muscle-bound doorman/bouncer, who let him through. Dan greets them friendlily, and they seem friendly right back
--SILENT PANEL

PANEL FOUR
On Amelia, trying to see what is on the other side of the door, but the door man or doormen step up, palms up, waving her away.

DOORMAN: Whoa whoa whoa, little lady.

DOORMAN: You don't look like one of the attendees, so if you ain't got an invitation, you ain't gettin' in.
***

Commission.

Commission.

JOHN LAYMAN

*The Kingdom of Badass just crowned its new King, and his name is "**Layman**."*

Layman has three cats: Rufus, Ash and Ruby. They are not badasses, though Ruby caught a lizard last week, and a hummingbird the week before.

*Enjoy his life's work at **Laymanlegoproject.tumblr.com***

ROB GUILLORY

Rob still lives and works in Lafayette, Louisiana. His studio lies in the shadow of the 50-foot shrine to George Rodrigue that locals have built out of alligator skins and rotting crawfish shells. There are many, many crackheads.

*Visit **RobGuillory.com** for all your sporadic blogging needs.*